The Doctor and The Death Moth

The Doctor and The Death Moth

Matthew Petchinsky

CONTENTS

The Doctor and The Death Moth
By Matthew Petchinsky

Disclaimer:

This story, *The Doctor and The Death Moth,* is a work of fan fiction. It is created for entertainment purposes only and is not affiliated with, endorsed by, or officially connected to the *Doctor Who* franchise or its creators. All characters, events, and elements of *Doctor Who* are the property of the BBC and their respective copyright holders. This story does not intend to infringe on any copyrights or trademarks. No profit is being made from this work, and it is purely a tribute to the *Doctor Who* universe and its fans.

Chapter 1: Arrival in the Shadow World

The TARDIS materialized with its familiar groaning sound, its blue wooden frame looking oddly out of place against the bleak landscape of the shadow world. The Doctor stepped out, his long coat flaring in the bitter wind, eyes scanning his surroundings with a mixture of caution and excitement.

"Well, this is... dreary," he muttered, tapping his fingers against the TARDIS's wooden surface. The air was thick with a mist that seemed to cling to everything, making it difficult to see more than a few feet ahead. The sky above was an unsettling swirl of grays and blacks, casting a dim light over the decaying world. The ground beneath his feet cracked and crumbled with each step, the earth dry and lifeless.

He adjusted his bow tie, a flicker of amusement on his face. "Curious. Very curious," he murmured, pulling out his sonic screwdriver. It whirred to life as he waved it around, the tip glowing a bright blue. "Strange energy signatures, temporal fluctuations, and... ah, what's this?" He squinted at the readout on the screwdriver, his brows knitting together in concern.

"This place is... alive," he whispered to himself, his voice barely carrying in the oppressive atmosphere. "But not in a way I've ever seen before." He took a few steps forward, eyes darting around, searching for signs of movement. The landscape was dotted with twisted, barren trees, their branches clawing at the sky like the gnarled fingers of a forgotten giant.

A chill ran down his spine. "Something's here," he said, more to himself than to the silent, shadowy world around him. "I can feel it."

The Doctor moved cautiously, his steps calculated as he made his way through the desolate terrain. He stopped suddenly, catching sight of something out of the corner of his eye—a flicker of motion in the distance. He turned sharply, squinting into the shadows, but saw nothing.

"Who's there?" he called out, his voice echoing through the still air. Silence answered him, an oppressive, almost tangible quiet. He took a deep breath, pushing aside the instinctive fear that crept up his spine.

"Right, play it cool," he muttered to himself. "You've faced down Daleks, Cybermen, even the Silence. Whatever's out here can't be that bad... can it?"

He continued to walk, his mind racing with possibilities. The temporal fluctuations were unlike anything he had encountered before. They pulsed through the air, a constant thrum that made his hearts beat a little faster. And there was something else—a presence. He could feel it, lurking just out of sight, observing his every move.

"Hello!" he called out again, his voice now laced with an edge of authority. "I'm the Doctor! I don't suppose you'd care for a friendly chat, would you?" The silence stretched on, and just as he was about to speak again, a faint rustling filled the air.

He froze, every nerve on high alert. The sound grew louder, like the fluttering of hundreds of wings, growing closer and closer. The Doctor's eyes widened as he peered into the mist. A dark shape emerged, shifting and morphing as it approached.

"Ah, there you are," he breathed, a mix of awe and apprehension in his voice. The shape solidified, revealing itself to be a creature unlike anything the Doctor had ever seen. It was massive, with wings that stretched out to either side, covered in what looked like scales that shimmered in the dim light. Its body was a twisting, ethereal mass of darkness, with glowing eyes that bore into him.

The Doctor took a cautious step back, eyes locked on the creature. "A moth... a giant, shadowy moth," he muttered, both fascinated and wary. "But you're not just any moth, are you? No, you're something much more... ancient." He slowly raised his sonic screwdriver, holding it out toward the creature.

The Death Moth remained silent, its wings creating a gust of wind that swept through the Doctor's hair. It hovered in place, its glowing eyes fixed on him with an intensity that made his skin crawl. Then, to his surprise, a voice echoed through his mind, cold and haunting.

"Why have you come here, Time Lord?"

The Doctor stiffened, eyes widening. "Telepathy! Of course, you're telepathic!" He grinned despite the situation, fascinated. "Well, hello there! I'm the Doctor, and I was just passing through when I noticed some... odd fluctuations. Thought I'd pop in and have a look around. You know how it is."

The Death Moth's eyes seemed to glow brighter, its form pulsing with an eerie light. *"This world is not for you,"* the voice intoned. *"It is the realm of decay, the boundary between life and death. Your presence disrupts the balance."*

"Ah, balance, is it?" The Doctor took a cautious step forward, trying to engage the creature. "Well, you see, I'm all for balance. Quite fond of it, actually. Keeps the universe ticking along nicely. But here's the thing—something's causing temporal disturbances here, and I can't just ignore that. It's what I do. I fix things." He gestured around him. "So, what exactly are you, then? A guardian? A... a Death Moth, maybe?"

"I am the harbinger of the end," the voice replied, a whisper that sent shivers through the air. *"Where there is imbalance, I bring order. Where there is life... I bring death."*

The Doctor felt a chill settle in his hearts. "Ah, well, that's a bit grim, isn't it?" he replied, forcing a smile. "Still, sounds like you're trying to do some good in your own way. But I can't let you go around destroying everything willy-nilly. There must be a reason for all this decay, and I'm going to find out what it is."

The Death Moth's wings fluttered, sending another gust of wind through the air. *"You cannot stop what has already begun, Doctor. The cycle must complete."*

The Doctor frowned, his mind racing. "Cycle? What cycle?" he demanded. "Is this world dying, or is it... evolving?" His eyes narrowed as he studied the creature, trying to piece together the clues.

The Death Moth remained silent, its form shimmering as if made of shadows and light. Then, without warning, it retreated into the darkness, disappearing into the mist with a final whisper that echoed in the Doctor's mind.

"Beware, Time Lord. The end draws near."

The Doctor stood there, staring into the shadows where the creature had vanished. "Well," he muttered, shoving his hands into his pockets. "This just got a whole lot more interesting." He turned back toward the TARDIS, his mind already whirring with possibilities. The Death Moth was a force of nature, a harbinger of some cosmic event that he didn't yet understand.

"But I will," he said to himself, determination hardening his gaze. "Oh, I will." With one last glance at the decaying world around him, he strode toward the TARDIS, ready to delve deeper into the mystery that lay ahead.

Little did he know, this encounter was only the beginning.

Chapter 2: Whispers in the Dark

The Doctor moved cautiously through the decaying landscape, his eyes scanning the horizon for any signs of life. The air was thick with an unsettling energy, the kind that made the hairs on the back of his neck stand on end. Every so often, he would catch a glimpse of movement in the shadows, but when he turned to look, there was nothing there.

"Definitely not a welcoming place," he muttered, pulling out his sonic screwdriver and giving it a wave. The device buzzed and clicked, lights flashing in rapid succession as it processed the environment around him. "Hmmm, interesting... very interesting." His expression shifted from concern to curiosity, his mind racing with possibilities.

After walking for what felt like hours, he came upon a series of large stone structures, half-buried in the ground and covered in moss. They loomed out of the fog like ancient sentinels, remnants of a civilization long forgotten. The Doctor approached cautiously, brushing his fingers along the weathered surface of one of the stones.

"Carvings," he murmured, eyes narrowing. The stone was etched with intricate symbols and strange writing. "This isn't just random rubble. These are ruins of a city... an old one, by the looks of it." His fingers traced the symbols, trying to decipher their meaning. The patterns seemed to tell a story—a cycle of life and death, of decay and rebirth. And central to every carving was the unmistakable image of a moth, its wings outstretched in a pose that was both majestic and terrifying.

"Ah, so you've been here for a while, haven't you?" The Doctor said, glancing around. "But where are the people? Every ruin has its story, and every story has its survivors... or witnesses."

As if on cue, a faint rustling filled the air, and the Doctor turned sharply. Out of the shadows, a figure emerged—a tall, gaunt man draped in tattered robes. His skin was pale, almost translucent, with eyes that glowed faintly in the dim light.

"Ah, there you are!" The Doctor exclaimed, a grin spreading across his face. "I was beginning to think this place was completely deserted."

The man regarded the Doctor warily, his eyes flickering with a mixture of fear and curiosity. "You... are not from this world," he said, his voice low and rasping.

"Very observant," the Doctor replied, taking a step closer. "I'm the Doctor. And you are...?"

The man hesitated, glancing around nervously before responding. "I am Kelnar, one of the Keepers of the Last Light." He bowed his head slightly, as if in deference to some unseen force. "You should not be here, Doctor. This place is cursed."

"Cursed, you say?" The Doctor's eyes lit up with interest. "By the Death Moth, I presume?"

Kelnar's face grew pale, and he shivered involuntarily at the mention of the creature. "Yes," he whispered. "The Death Moth brings destruction to all it touches. It is a force of nature, an entity that exists to maintain the balance of life and death. We, the remnants of our people, live in its shadow, praying that we do not attract its wrath."

The Doctor crossed his arms, frowning. "Interesting. So, it doesn't just indiscriminately destroy? It... chooses its targets?"

Kelnar nodded, his gaze distant. "It comes when the balance is disrupted, when life grows beyond what is meant to be. The Death Moth brings death to restore equilibrium. Those who have tried to fight it, to control it, have all perished."

"And yet you're still here," the Doctor pointed out, raising an eyebrow. "Which means there's more to this story, isn't there? How have you managed to survive its wrath for so long?"

"We survive because we do not interfere," Kelnar replied solemnly. "We have learned to live in harmony with the world, taking only what we need and giving back when we can. The Death Moth does not seek us because we respect the cycle of life."

The Doctor tapped his chin thoughtfully. "So, it's not just a mindless force of destruction. It has... rules. A code, even. Fascinating." His eyes brightened with a sudden idea. "Tell me, Kelnar, is there a place where I might learn more about this creature? Some ancient texts or records, perhaps?"

Kelnar hesitated, looking around nervously as if afraid they were being watched. "There are legends," he said slowly, "written in the Old Temple. But it is forbidden to enter."

"Forbidden, you say?" The Doctor grinned mischievously. "Well, those are my favorite kinds of places! Lead the way, Kelnar."

"No!" Kelnar hissed, stepping back. "You do not understand! The Old Temple is a place of death. Many who enter do not return. The Death Moth guards its secrets fiercely."

"Well, that's never stopped me before," the Doctor replied with a shrug. "Besides, how can we hope to understand it, to help it even, if we don't try to learn? There's always a way, Kelnar. Always."

Kelnar seemed to waver, his gaze searching the Doctor's face for any sign of doubt. Finding none, he sighed and nodded. "Very well. I will show you the path, but I will not enter. If you choose to go, you do so at your own peril."

"Deal!" The Doctor replied cheerfully, clapping his hands together. "Lead on, my friend."

They walked in silence for a time, the path winding through the ruins of the ancient city. The buildings, though in various states of decay, still bore signs of their former grandeur. Pillars adorned with intricate carvings lined the streets, and statues of beings with moth-like wings loomed overhead, casting eerie shadows on the ground.

Kelnar led the Doctor to a large structure at the edge of the city. Its walls were covered in symbols and runes, and a massive archway stood open, leading into darkness.

"The Old Temple," Kelnar said quietly, his voice tinged with fear. "Inside, you will find the writings of our ancestors, the ones who first encountered the Death Moth. But be warned, Doctor: the shadows are alive in that place. They will test you."

The Doctor nodded, his face set in determination. "Thank you, Kelnar. I'll be fine. Just stay out here, and if anything comes flapping out of there that's not me, run the other way, alright?"

Kelnar managed a weak smile. "May the light protect you, Doctor."

With that, the Doctor turned and stepped into the darkness of the temple. The air inside was cold, filled with a faint, buzzing hum that seemed to come from everywhere at once. His eyes adjusted slowly to the dim light, and he could make out the shapes of stone pillars and walls covered in ancient writing.

"Now, let's see what secrets you're hiding," he murmured, pulling out his sonic screwdriver to illuminate the carvings on the walls. The symbols told a story of a world in balance, of life flourishing under the light of a bright star. But then, the balance tipped. The creatures depicted on the walls grew larger, more numerous, until the star itself began to wane.

And then came the moth.

In every panel that followed, the Death Moth was present, bringing darkness and decay. But amidst the destruction, new life emerged—different, adapted to the changed world. The carvings seemed to suggest that the Death Moth was not a bringer of doom, but a force of transformation, ensuring that life could continue, even in altered forms.

"Ah-ha!" The Doctor exclaimed, eyes gleaming with excitement. "You're not just a destroyer; you're a catalyst for change. A bit harsh, but effective." He ran his fingers over the final carving, which depicted the moth with its wings outstretched, surrounded by a swirling mass of light and shadow.

"Fascinating," he breathed. "You don't bring death for its own sake. You bring it to make way for something new. But why now? Why here?" He stepped back, deep in thought. "What's disturbed the balance this time?"

Suddenly, a faint whisper filled the air, echoing through the chamber. The Doctor turned sharply, holding up his sonic screwdriver. "Who's there?" he called out.

The whisper grew louder, forming into words. *"You seek to understand... but understanding comes at a price."*

The Doctor narrowed his eyes, his hearts pounding in his chest. "I'm willing to pay it," he replied, his voice firm. "Show yourself."

The air around him shimmered, and for a brief moment, the outline of the Death Moth appeared before him, its eyes glowing in the darkness. *"Beware, Doctor. Knowledge is a double-edged sword. You cannot stop the cycle, only witness it."*

And with that, the presence vanished, leaving the Doctor alone in the temple's dark, echoing halls.

"Right," he muttered, tucking his sonic screwdriver into his pocket. "Witness it, then. But I'll find a way to make sure that cycle doesn't just end in destruction. Not this time." He turned and headed back toward the entrance, ready to face whatever challenges awaited him outside.

The mystery of the Death Moth was deeper than he'd thought, but now he had a direction—a path to follow. And if there was one thing the Doctor excelled at, it was uncovering the truth.

Chapter 3: The First Encounter

The Doctor emerged from the Old Temple, the words of the Death Moth still echoing in his mind. The oppressive atmosphere of the shadow world pressed in on him once again, the darkness thicker and the air colder than before. Kelnar stood waiting at the entrance, his eyes widening as the Doctor approached.

"You... you returned," Kelnar stammered, his voice a mixture of awe and disbelief. "I feared you would be lost like the others."

"Not today," the Doctor replied, his tone sharp with determination. "I've learned quite a bit, but there are still pieces missing. The Death Moth, Kelnar, it's not just a destroyer. It's a force of transformation, but there's more to it. Something else is driving it, something it's responding to."

Kelnar nodded slowly, his gaze dropping to the ground. "The balance has been disrupted," he muttered, almost to himself. "We can feel it, the pulse of life here growing weaker with every passing day."

The Doctor nodded thoughtfully, ready to press Kelnar further when he heard a sound in the distance—a low, rhythmic thud that vibrated through the earth beneath their feet. His eyes snapped up, scanning the horizon. "No..." he muttered, a chill creeping up his spine.

"What is it?" Kelnar asked, fear edging into his voice.

"Trouble," the Doctor replied, his face grim. "Big, metal, very extermination-focused trouble."

The sound grew louder, punctuated by mechanical grinding and the faint hum of energy weapons. From the shadows emerged a group of Cybermen, their eyes glowing a cold, metallic blue as they marched forward in perfect unison. The Doctor's hearts skipped a beat at the sight.

"Cybermen," he whispered, taking a step back. "But how did they get here? And more importantly, why are they here?"

Kelnar's face drained of color as he stumbled backward, staring in horror at the approaching figures. "The Death Moth... it will come," he stammered. "It always comes when they arrive."

"Wait, wait!" the Doctor called out, raising a hand to Kelnar as he stepped forward, trying to remain calm despite the rising tension. "We need to understand this before we panic. Cybermen are a bit of a problem, yes, but if the Death Moth is going to make an appearance..."

As if in response to his words, the air grew cold and still. A low, buzzing hum filled the atmosphere, like the sound of a thousand wings beating in unison. The Doctor looked up, his eyes scanning the dark sky. "It's here," he breathed, a mix of dread and fascination in his voice.

The Cybermen came to a halt, their heads swiveling in perfect synchronization toward the source of the sound. "Unidentified entity detected," one of them droned, its voice hollow and mechanical. "Prepare for elimination."

"No, no, no, this is bad," the Doctor muttered, pulling out his sonic screwdriver and waving it around frantically. "You don't know what you're dealing with! You need to back off—"

The Doctor's warning was cut short by a sudden burst of light. From the sky descended a storm of glowing wings and swirling shadows, coalescing into a massive, ethereal shape. The Death Moth appeared, its wings stretching wide, shimmering with an otherworldly radiance. It hovered above the Cybermen, a pulsating mass of darkness and light, its eyes glowing with an intense, almost blinding brilliance.

"Cybermen, listen to me!" the Doctor shouted, his voice strained with urgency. "You need to retreat! Now!"

But the Cybermen were not known for retreating. They raised their arm-mounted weapons, aiming them at the Death Moth. "Target acquired," one intoned. "Initiating extermination protocol."

A high-pitched whine filled the air as the Cybermen fired in unison, beams of energy streaking toward the Death Moth. For a split second, it seemed like the moth would be overwhelmed, but then it moved. Its wings beat once, and a wave of darkness surged out, swallowing the energy blasts whole.

"Fascinating," the Doctor breathed, his eyes wide with awe. "It absorbed the energy... like it's feeding off of it."

The Cybermen hesitated for a moment, their programming struggling to comprehend what had just happened. Then, they recalibrated, readying their weapons for another volley. But the Death Moth was faster. It descended in a blur of light and shadow, its wings stretching wide. With a single beat, a shockwave of dark energy erupted from its body, crashing into the Cybermen like a tidal wave.

"No!" the Doctor shouted, raising his arm as if to shield himself from the blast. The ground trembled, the air crackling with raw power as the shockwave struck the Cybermen. They were lifted off their feet, their metal bodies twisting and contorting under the immense force. Sparks flew, and the Doctor heard the screech of tearing metal as the Cybermen were ripped apart, their fragments scattering across the landscape.

When the dust settled, the Cybermen lay in pieces, their once-imposing forms reduced to twisted, broken remnants. The Death Moth hovered above them, its eyes glowing with an eerie, pulsating light. It had destroyed them effortlessly, with a power that was both terrifying and mesmerizing.

The Doctor stood frozen, his mind racing to process what he had just witnessed. "You... you didn't just destroy them," he muttered, eyes fixed on the Death Moth. "You... disassembled them, unraveled their very essence."

The Death Moth turned its gaze toward the Doctor, its eyes boring into him. For a moment, he felt a cold grip around his hearts, an indescribable presence pressing into his consciousness.

"Who are you?" the Doctor whispered, his voice barely audible. "What are you really?"

"I am the end," a voice echoed in his mind, cold and ancient. *"I am the harbinger of balance. Where there is disruption, I bring order. You, Time Lord, are an anomaly. Why do you seek to understand?"*

"Because that's what I do!" the Doctor shot back, his fear giving way to defiance. "I'm the Doctor, and I make it my business to understand the universe, to help where I can! And you... you're not just some mindless force of destruction. I can see it now—you're... sentient, intelligent. You have a purpose, but why? Why this world? Why now?"

The Death Moth remained silent, its form flickering like a candle in the wind. Then, slowly, it began to descend, touching down on the ground a few feet away from the Doctor. Its wings folded around its body, creating a cloak of darkness that shimmered with the faint glow of its inner light.

"The cycle has begun," it intoned, its voice reverberating through the Doctor's mind. *"This world has grown beyond its time. The balance must be restored."*

The Doctor took a cautious step forward, his eyes locked on the creature. "You say balance, but whose balance? Who decides when a world has grown beyond its time? Is it you? Or is there something... someone else?" His voice softened, pleading. "There must be another way. A way that doesn't end in death and destruction."

The Death Moth shifted, its eyes narrowing as it regarded him. For a brief moment, the Doctor sensed something behind the creature's cold, calculated presence—a hint of sadness, of conflict. But it vanished as quickly as it appeared, replaced by an unyielding resolve.

"The cycle cannot be altered," it said, its tone final. *"To interfere is to invite greater chaos. You, Doctor, must accept this truth or be consumed by it."*

With that, the Death Moth spread its wings wide, a gust of wind swirling around it. The shadows darkened, the air growing colder as it began to ascend once more, its form becoming indistinct, like smoke dissolving into the night sky.

"Wait!" the Doctor called out, but it was too late. The Death Moth disappeared into the darkness, leaving behind only the scattered remnants of the Cybermen and a profound silence that settled over the world.

The Doctor stood there, his hearts heavy, his mind buzzing with questions. "It has rules," he muttered to himself, his gaze fixed on the spot where the Death Moth had vanished. "A code, a purpose. It's not just destruction—it's balance, transformation. But who defines that balance? And why now?"

He turned back to the ruins, his expression grim but resolute. "I'm going to find out," he vowed, clenching his fists. "No more death, not if I can help it."

With one last glance at the darkened sky, he strode back toward the temple and Kelnar, the path ahead uncertain but clear in his mind. This was only the beginning, and he was determined to uncover the truth behind the Death Moth—before it was too late.

Chapter 4: Secrets of the Death Moth

The darkness of the ancient city was palpable as the Doctor made his way back to Kelnar, who was still waiting at the temple entrance. His face was pale, eyes wide with fear. "You saw it, didn't you?" Kelnar asked, his voice a hushed whisper. "The Death Moth... it came."

The Doctor nodded grimly. "Yes, I saw it. And it's not just a mindless force. There's intelligence there, purpose, even a sort of... code it follows." He took a deep breath, his gaze shifting to the ground as his mind raced with possibilities. "There's more to this than what meets the eye. I need to find out everything I can about that creature."

Kelnar looked at him with a mix of fear and confusion. "The legends say that the Death Moth guards the ancient secrets. They are hidden deep within the planet, in the Chamber of Balance."

"The Chamber of Balance?" The Doctor's eyes lit up with interest. "Now we're getting somewhere. Where is this chamber?"

"It lies deep in the heart of the world," Kelnar replied, his gaze dropping to the ground. "It's a place of death, where only the keepers of the ancient knowledge can tread. Few have returned after entering its depths, and those who did were... changed."

"Well," the Doctor said, his tone light despite the gravity of the situation, "luckily, I have a knack for poking around in places I shouldn't. So, this chamber—how do I get there?"

Kelnar hesitated, his gaze flickering with fear. "The path is treacherous," he warned. "It lies beneath the Great Spire in the center of the city. A labyrinth of tunnels leads down to the core, where the Chamber of Balance resides."

"Perfect!" The Doctor clapped his hands together, his eyes gleaming with excitement. "The Great Spire it is, then!" He turned on his heel and began striding purposefully through the ruins, leaving Kelnar to hurry after him.

The journey to the Great Spire was a winding path through crumbling streets and dilapidated buildings. The Doctor's mind raced with questions: what was the true purpose of the Death Moth? Why did it seem to target only certain entities? He had to know, and the Chamber of Balance seemed to be his best chance at answers.

The spire itself was an immense structure, its surface carved with symbols and runes that glowed faintly in the darkness. At its base was a circular doorway, covered in ancient glyphs. The Doctor ran his fingers over the carvings, feeling the faint hum of energy beneath his touch.

"This is it," he murmured, pulling out his sonic screwdriver. "The entrance to the chamber. Let's see if we can convince it to let us in, shall we?" He aimed the screwdriver at the doorway, and it emitted a high-pitched whine as it scanned the symbols.

For a moment, nothing happened. Then, slowly, the symbols began to shift and glow, forming an intricate pattern across the door's surface. With a low rumble, the door slid open, revealing a dark tunnel leading deep into the planet.

"Brilliant!" the Doctor exclaimed, flashing Kelnar a grin. "Looks like we're in business. Now, stay close, and don't touch anything you're not supposed to."

Kelnar nodded, swallowing nervously as they descended into the tunnel. The air grew colder and denser as they made their way through the labyrinthine passages, the darkness pressing in on them from all sides. Strange carvings lined the walls, depicting scenes of cosmic events, creatures, and worlds being born and destroyed.

"These carvings," the Doctor said, holding up his screwdriver to illuminate them, "they're telling a story. A cycle of creation and destruction, like the one we saw in the temple."

Kelnar nodded. "The stories of our ancestors say that the Death Moth was created by the universe itself, to act as its guardian."

The Doctor's eyes narrowed as he examined one of the carvings, which showed the Death Moth standing amidst a field of stars. "A guardian," he muttered. "A creature of balance... but balance for what?"

They continued deeper until they reached a vast, circular chamber at the heart of the labyrinth. The room was filled with towering stone pillars, each one etched with symbols that glowed faintly in the dim light. At the center stood a large pedestal, upon which rested a massive, stone tablet covered in ancient writing.

"This must be it," the Doctor said, his voice echoing slightly in the chamber. "The Chamber of Balance." He approached the pedestal, his eyes scanning the tablet. "Let's see what secrets you're hiding."

The Doctor reached out and traced the symbols with his fingers. The tablet seemed to pulse under his touch, the glow of the symbols intensifying. Slowly, words began to form in his mind, ancient and cryptic but understandable.

"It's a history," the Doctor murmured, his eyes wide with fascination. "The story of the Death Moth... and its purpose."

Kelnar watched in silence as the Doctor began to read aloud. "The Death Moth," he translated, "was created in the dawn of the universe, forged from the very fabric of reality to maintain balance. Its purpose is to eliminate that which defies the natural order... to destroy what grows beyond its time."

His eyes moved to another section of the tablet. "It is drawn to anomalies, things that upset the cosmic balance. Like a cosmic predator, it hunts down those who threaten the equilibrium of the universe."

"Then... it is here because of the Cybermen?" Kelnar asked, his voice trembling.

"Not just them," the Doctor replied, his voice grim. "Anything that threatens the natural order. The Daleks, the Cybermen... they are unnatural, perversions of life that seek to dominate, to consume everything in their path. The Death Moth sees them as a threat to the balance and seeks to eliminate them."

He paused, his fingers brushing over the symbols. "But there's more," he continued, his voice dropping to a whisper. "The Death Moth does not act on its own. It follows a higher command, a cosmic will, ensuring that life continues but within the bounds of the natural order."

Kelnar took a step back, his face pale. "Then... there is no stopping it," he breathed. "It will destroy all that defies the balance."

"Not quite," the Doctor replied, his eyes narrowing as he studied the final lines of the tablet. "There is a way to change its course, to alter its path. The key lies in understanding the balance it seeks to maintain."

"And how do we do that?" Kelnar asked, desperation creeping into his voice.

The Doctor turned to face him, his eyes blazing with determination. "We show it that the balance can be restored without destruction. The Death Moth is not mindless; it follows rules, a code. If we can demonstrate that there is another way to maintain the balance, it might—just might—change its course."

Kelnar shook his head, fear and doubt etched across his features. "But how can we, mere mortals, change the will of such a force?"

The Doctor smiled faintly, his gaze turning back to the tablet. "We do what we always do, Kelnar. We try. We use our knowledge, our willpower, and our hope. The universe is not a cold machine; it's alive, filled with possibilities. The Death Moth may be a force of balance, but even forces of nature can be reasoned with if you know how."

He turned away from the pedestal and began walking back toward the entrance of the chamber. "Now, we need to find the Death Moth again," he said over his shoulder. "And this time, we're going to talk."

Kelnar hesitated before following, his mind a whirlwind of thoughts. "Do you truly believe it will listen?" he asked quietly.

"I have to believe it will," the Doctor replied, his voice firm. "Because if it doesn't, then there's only one path left—destruction. And I'm not ready to let that happen. Not here, not now."

As they made their way back through the labyrinth, the Doctor's mind was ablaze with plans and theories. The Death Moth was a creature of balance, a cosmic enforcer—but it wasn't beyond understanding. He had glimpsed its purpose, its drive to maintain equilibrium in the universe. Now, he needed to convince it that balance could be restored without ending everything it touched.

The journey ahead was uncertain, but one thing was clear: the Doctor had to find a way to alter the course of the Death Moth's wrath. And if anyone could do it, it was him. Because if the universe had taught him anything, it was that even in the darkest of times, there was always a glimmer of hope, a chance to rewrite the rules.

And he was ready to take that chance.

Chapter 5: The Arrival of the Daleks

The Doctor and Kelnar emerged from the depths of the labyrinth, the echoes of the Chamber of Balance still fresh in their minds. The oppressive darkness of the shadow world hung heavily around them, the air thick with tension. The Doctor strode forward with a sense of urgency, his mind whirring with possibilities. He knew he needed to find the Death Moth again—but this time, it would be to reason with it, to show that balance could be achieved without rampant destruction.

However, the universe had other plans.

A low, rhythmic thrum suddenly filled the air, vibrating through the ground beneath their feet. The Doctor halted in his tracks, his eyes narrowing. "No... that sound," he muttered, turning sharply toward the horizon. "It can't be."

Kelnar froze beside him, his face paling. "What is it?" he asked, a tremor of fear creeping into his voice.

"Trouble," the Doctor replied grimly, his gaze fixed on a distant, dim glow growing brighter with each second. "Metallic, genocidal trouble." He turned to Kelnar, eyes blazing with intensity. "You need to hide. Now."

"But what about—" Kelnar began, but the Doctor cut him off, his tone sharp.

"Just go!" he snapped, already reaching into his coat for his sonic screwdriver. "I'll handle this." Without waiting for Kelnar's reply, the Doctor broke into a sprint, heading toward the source of the noise. His hearts pounded in his chest, a mix of fear and anger coursing through his veins. He knew that sound all too well.

Daleks.

As he neared the edge of the city ruins, he caught sight of them—rows of gleaming, armored shells, gliding smoothly across the decaying landscape. The Daleks moved in perfect formation, their eye-stalks swiveling back and forth as they scanned their surroundings. In the dim light of the shadow world, their metallic casings glinted with an eerie, ominous sheen.

"Of course, it's the Daleks," the Doctor muttered under his breath, his expression hardening. "They never miss a chance to poke their eye-stalks where they don't belong."

He ducked behind a fallen pillar, watching as the Dalek squadron advanced, their leader gliding forward. This particular Dalek was adorned with a series of symbols and markings across its casing—a Dalek Commander, no doubt. It stopped, its eyestalk swiveling to survey the ruins.

"COMMENCE SCAN!" the Dalek Commander ordered in its grating, metallic voice. "LOCATE THE DEATH MOTH! ITS POWER MUST BE HARNESSSED FOR THE DALEK EMPIRE!"

The other Daleks fanned out, their gunsticks pointed forward as they scanned the area. The Doctor bit his lip, his mind racing. They had followed him here, somehow tracking the temporal fluctuations of the Death Moth to this world. And now, they sought to control that power for their own purposes.

"This is bad," the Doctor muttered, rubbing his temple as he considered his next move. "Very, very bad." He needed to act fast, but he had to be careful. If the Daleks provoked the Death Moth, the consequences could be catastrophic.

"INITIATE PROBING PROTOCOL!" the Dalek Commander screeched. "THE DEATH MOTH WILL BE LOCATED AND CONTAINED!"

The Daleks began to spread out, their scanning devices buzzing and whirring as they probed the ruins. The Doctor peeked out from behind the pillar, his mind racing. He couldn't let the Daleks get to the Death Moth. Not only would they try to exploit its power, but their very presence was already disrupting the balance the Death Moth sought to protect.

"Right, time to intervene," the Doctor muttered to himself. He adjusted his bow tie, took a deep breath, and stepped out into the open. "Oi! Daleks!" he called, waving his arms. "Over here! You're looking for something, yes?"

The Dalek Commander swiveled its eyestalk toward him, the blue light at its tip intensifying. "THE DOCTOR!" it shrieked, its voice rising in pitch. "THE DOCTOR HAS BEEN LOCATED! EXTERMINATE!"

The other Daleks turned, their gunsticks aiming directly at the Doctor. But he stood his ground, raising his hands in a gesture of mock surrender. "Ah, there you are," he said casually, his voice dripping with sarcasm. "How wonderful to see you again. And by wonderful, I mean absolutely dreadful."

"YOU WILL BE EXTERMINATED!" the Dalek Commander screamed, its casing vibrating with the intensity of its shout.

"Yes, yes, I get it," the Doctor replied, rolling his eyes. "Exterminate this, exterminate that. But before you go blasting me into atoms, let's have a little chat, shall we? You see, you're making a very big mistake."

"EXPLAIN!" the Dalek barked, its eyestalk fixed on the Doctor.

The Doctor took a step forward, his expression serious. "The Death Moth," he said, his tone grave. "It's not something you can control. It's a force of balance, designed to eliminate anything that disrupts the natural order—including you."

"DALEKS DO NOT FEAR THE DEATH MOTH!" the Commander shrieked. "THE POWER OF THE DEATH MOTH WILL BE ADDED TO THE DALEK EMPIRE!"

The Doctor shook his head, frustration etched on his face. "You just don't get it, do you? The Death Moth is here because of you! It's drawn to entities like the Daleks that upset the balance. It's not a tool to be used; it's a force to be respected."

"IRRELEVANT!" the Dalek Commander screeched. "DALEKS WILL CONQUER! DALEKS WILL CONTROL!"

The Doctor clenched his fists, anger bubbling up inside him. "You're meddling with forces you don't understand," he snapped. "And if you push it too far, it will destroy you."

"THEN THE DOCTOR WILL BE DESTROYED FIRST!" the Dalek Commander declared, its gunstick charging with energy. "PREPARE FOR EXTERMINATION!"

But before the Dalek could fire, a sudden gust of wind swept through the ruins, carrying with it a faint, rhythmic buzzing sound—the unmistakable hum of beating wings. The Doctor's eyes widened, and he took a step back, his hearts pounding in his chest.

"No," he whispered. "It's too soon. It's already here."

From the shadows above, a brilliant glow appeared, growing in intensity. The air grew colder, and the darkness seemed to swirl around a central point as the Death Moth descended in a storm of light and shadow. Its wings spread wide, their edges glinting with an eerie, ethereal light.

"WARNING!" the Dalek Commander shrieked, its eyestalk swiveling toward the glowing figure. "UNKNOWN ENTITY DETECTED! INITIATE CONTAINMENT PROTOCOL!"

The Daleks raised their weapons, their gunsticks sparking as they charged up. But before they could fire, the Death Moth moved. Its wings beat once, sending a shockwave of dark energy crashing into the Daleks. The Doctor shielded his face as the force of the blast swept past him, the ground trembling beneath his feet.

The Daleks were thrown back, their metal casings screeching as they skidded across the ground. Sparks flew, and the Doctor heard the sound of metal crumpling and tearing. The Daleks tried to recover, their gunsticks flaring with energy, but the Death Moth struck again. A wave of shadows engulfed them, and in an instant, their casings began to collapse inward, crushed by an unseen force.

"RETREAT!" the Dalek Commander screeched, its voice now filled with something the Doctor had never heard from a Dalek before—fear. "RETREAT! THE ENTITY CANNOT BE CONTAINED!"

But it was too late. The Death Moth surged forward, its form twisting and expanding as it enveloped the Daleks. The Doctor watched, both horrified and fascinated, as the Daleks' metal shells crumpled like paper under the moth's power. A brilliant flash of light erupted from the center of the storm, and then... silence.

When the light faded, the Daleks were gone, their remains scattered across the ground like the broken fragments of a terrible dream. The Death Moth hovered above the ruins, its wings still glowing with that otherworldly light. It turned, its gaze falling on the Doctor, who stood frozen in place.

"Well," the Doctor muttered, his voice shaky but defiant. "That was... quite the display."

The Death Moth did not respond, but he could feel its presence pressing into his mind. Cold, ancient, and yet... questioning.

"Do you see now?" the Doctor said, taking a step forward. "They're gone, yes, but what have you achieved? Balance isn't just about destruction. It's about finding a way for life to thrive without tearing everything apart."

The Death Moth's eyes flickered, its form rippling as if caught in a struggle. For a moment, the Doctor sensed something beneath the cold exterior—a hint of understanding, or perhaps doubt.

"You don't have to do this," he continued, his voice steady despite the tension in the air. "There's another way. Let me help you find it."

The Death Moth remained silent, its wings beating slowly as it hovered above the ruins. Then, without a sound, it turned and began to ascend, dissolving into the darkness of the sky.

The Doctor watched it go, his shoulders sagging with exhaustion. "Well," he muttered, rubbing his temples, "that went about as well as I expected."

He turned and began to walk back toward the city, his mind racing. The Daleks had been destroyed, but that was only a temporary fix. The Death Moth was still out there, its purpose clear but its path uncertain. And now, the Doctor had to find a way to change its course before it brought about more destruction.

As he walked, he couldn't help but glance over his shoulder at the sky, where the Death Moth had vanished. "This isn't over," he said softly. "Not by a long shot."

Chapter 6: Cybermen's Last Stand

The Doctor stood amidst the ruins, his gaze fixed on the sky where the Death Moth had vanished. His hearts were still pounding from the encounter with the Daleks and the terrible power of the moth. The landscape was littered with the broken remnants of the Daleks, their once-mighty casings now twisted fragments glinting in the dim light of the shadow world.

A sudden, harsh mechanical whirring filled the air behind him. The Doctor spun around, his eyes widening as several battered figures emerged from the shadows. Their metal bodies bore the unmistakable marks of recent combat—dents, scorch marks, missing limbs. It was the Cybermen, the survivors from the earlier encounter.

"Ah," the Doctor said, straightening up, his voice a mix of irritation and curiosity. "You lot survived, did you?"

The lead Cyberman stepped forward, its movements stiff and jerky. Its left arm hung uselessly by its side, sparks occasionally flickering from the exposed wiring. "We... survived," it intoned, its voice distorted and halting. "The Daleks... have been... eliminated."

"Yes, I noticed," the Doctor replied, crossing his arms. "All thanks to our friend, the Death Moth. And let me guess, you're not here for tea and a friendly chat, are you?"

"Negative," the Cyberman replied. "The entity poses... a threat... to Cyber-kind."

"Well, that's an understatement," the Doctor muttered, rubbing his temple. "It's a threat to anything that disrupts the balance of the universe, including you Cybermen. So, what's the plan? Gonna try and delete it?"

There was a moment of silence, and the Cybermen stood eerily still, their mechanical minds processing the situation. "We propose... an alliance," the lead Cyberman finally stated. "Temporary. To neutralize the threat."

The Doctor raised an eyebrow, a hint of a smile tugging at the corners of his mouth. "An alliance, you say? With the Cybermen? My, my, things really are dire, aren't they?" He turned away, pacing as he thought aloud. "And what makes you think I'd agree to this little team-up of yours?"

"Survival," the Cyberman replied bluntly. "The Death Moth threatens all. You possess... knowledge. Together, we may find a way... to neutralize the entity."

The Doctor stopped pacing, turning to face the Cybermen. "Neutralize it?" he repeated, his tone darkening. "The Death Moth isn't something you can just turn off or blast to pieces. It's a force of nature, a part of the cosmic order. If you go in guns blazing, you'll end up just like the Daleks."

"Then... you will assist," the Cyberman stated, its tone indicating not a request, but a demand.

The Doctor narrowed his eyes, the gears in his mind turning rapidly. The Cybermen were cold, calculating machines. They wouldn't propose an alliance unless they genuinely feared the threat. And he needed to understand more about the Death Moth's purpose and origins if he was to have any chance of stopping it.

"Alright," he said finally, his voice firm. "I'll help you. But on my terms. No destroying or attempting to control the Death Moth. We study it, understand it, and figure out what exactly has caused this... imbalance it seeks to correct. Deal?"

The Cyberman's eyepiece glowed as it processed his words. "Agreed," it intoned. "Temporary... alliance."

"Right," the Doctor muttered, turning on his heel. "Follow me then. We're going back to the Old Temple."

As they made their way back through the ruins, the Cybermen moved in eerie silence, their footsteps heavy and metallic. The Doctor's mind raced with thoughts of what lay ahead. He had now, somewhat reluctantly, allied himself with one of his oldest enemies. Yet, in the face of the Death Moth's overwhelming power, it seemed the only way forward.

They arrived at the Old Temple, its dark, looming entrance as foreboding as ever. The Doctor glanced over his shoulder at the Cybermen. "This is where we start," he said, pointing at the entrance. "The carvings inside provide clues about the Death Moth's origins and purpose. I'll translate them; you keep an eye out for any... unexpected visitors."

The Cybermen gave a stiff nod, their weapons at the ready as they took up positions around the entrance. The Doctor entered the temple, his sonic screwdriver illuminating the dim interior. Kelnar, who had been waiting anxiously inside, stepped forward as the Doctor approached.

"Doctor!" he exclaimed, his eyes widening as he caught sight of the Cybermen outside. "What have you done? You brought them here?"

"Temporary truce," the Doctor replied curtly, kneeling by one of the ancient carvings on the wall. "We need all the help we can get if we're to understand the Death Moth and what it's doing here."

Kelnar's expression twisted with fear and disbelief, but he remained silent, watching as the Doctor began to study the carvings. The symbols seemed to glow faintly in the light of the sonic screwdriver, revealing more of the story they told.

"These symbols," the Doctor muttered, tracing his fingers over the stone. "They speak of balance, cycles of creation and destruction. The Death Moth is drawn to worlds where the natural order has been disrupted, where life is twisted into something unnatural."

He glanced at Kelnar, his eyes intense. "This world, your world, has been a target for both the Daleks and the Cybermen—two species that epitomize the perversion of life's balance. The Daleks, bent on extermination and domination. The Cybermen, striving for a 'perfection' that strips away all individuality and life."

Kelnar nodded, his face pale. "Then... the Death Moth is here to cleanse this world of their influence."

"Yes," the Doctor replied, his voice grim. "But it's not that simple. The moth isn't just targeting them; it's targeting everything it perceives as part of the imbalance. That includes your people, Kelnar."

"The solution...?" the lead Cyberman asked from the entrance, its gaze fixed on the Doctor.

The Doctor sighed, standing up and facing the mechanical figures. "We have to understand its code, its rules. Every force of nature has a set of guidelines it follows. If we can figure out what specific imbalance the Death Moth is reacting to, we might be able to convince it to halt its rampage or at least divert its attention."

"DATA... REQUIRED," the Cyberman stated, its voice grating and hollow. "WE MUST ACCESS... THE CORE OF THE ENTITY'S POWER."

"Exactly," the Doctor replied, nodding. "We need to find the source of its power. The carvings here indicate that deep within this world, there exists a... nexus of energy, a place where the Death Moth draws its strength. We need to get there."

Kelnar's eyes widened in horror. "The Heart of Shadows," he whispered. "It lies in the deepest cavern beneath the planet's surface. No one who has entered has ever returned."

"Then it's exactly where we need to go," the Doctor said, his tone decisive. "If we're to have any hope of communicating with the Death Moth and understanding its true purpose, we need to confront it at its source."

"RISK... ACCEPTABLE," the lead Cyberman replied, stepping forward. "WE WILL... PROCEED."

"Good," the Doctor replied curtly, turning to face the dark passage leading deeper into the planet. "But remember, this is a reconnaissance mission. We're not here to destroy or control. We're here to understand."

The Cybermen fell in line behind the Doctor as they began their descent into the cavernous depths of the planet. The air grew colder and denser, and the walls around them pulsed with a faint, otherworldly light. The path wound downward in a spiral, the darkness pressing in from all sides.

They walked in silence for what felt like hours, the only sounds the clank of the Cybermen's feet and the Doctor's occasional mutterings as he scanned the surroundings with his sonic screwdriver. Kelnar followed closely behind, his expression a mixture of fear and determination.

Finally, they reached the end of the path. Before them lay a vast chamber, its walls lined with glowing symbols similar to those in the Old Temple. At the center of the chamber was a swirling vortex of light and shadow—a nexus of energy that radiated an almost unbearable pressure.

"The Heart of Shadows," the Doctor breathed, his eyes wide as he approached the edge of the vortex. "This is where the Death Moth draws its power. A connection point between this world and the fabric of the universe itself."

"SCANNING," the lead Cyberman intoned, raising its arm and directing a beam of light toward the vortex. "ENERGY SIGNATURE... CONSISTENT WITH ENTITY. ANALYSIS... INCOMPLETE."

The Doctor knelt beside the vortex, his gaze intense as he studied the swirling mass of energy. "It's not just a source of power," he murmured. "It's a gateway—a bridge between the natural order and the imbalance it seeks to correct. The Death Moth is tied to this world, reacting to its state of disorder."

Kelnar stepped forward, his face pale. "Then... it will not stop until everything it perceives as a threat is eradicated."

"Not necessarily," the Doctor replied, standing up and turning to face his companions. "If we can alter the parameters it uses to judge the balance, we might be able to convince it that this world is no longer a threat. We need to send a signal through this nexus—a message that shows the balance can be restored without further destruction."

"AND IF IT... DOES NOT ACCEPT?" the Cyberman asked, its gaze fixed on the swirling vortex.

"Then," the Doctor said softly, his expression darkening, "we'll be out of options. But I have to believe that there's another way, that the Death Moth can be reasoned with."

He turned back to the vortex, raising his sonic screwdriver. "Let's get to work," he muttered, his voice steely. "The fate of this world, and possibly the universe, depends on it."

And so, in the heart of the shadow world, an unlikely alliance began its desperate attempt to communicate with the Death Moth, to show it that balance could be restored without the obliteration of everything in its path. But the clock was ticking, and the darkness around them grew ever deeper, as if the world itself was waiting to see if the Doctor could succeed... or if the Death Moth would carry out its grim task to the bitter end.

Chapter 7: The Power of the Death Moth

The chamber pulsed with an eerie light as the Doctor and his unlikely allies stood before the swirling nexus at the heart of the shadow world. The air hummed with a strange energy, and the ground beneath them seemed to tremble in the presence of the vortex. The Doctor felt the intense pressure in his chest, like a heartbeat that echoed through the room. He could feel the power of the Death Moth in every fiber of his being, a force both terrifying and awe-inspiring.

"We need to understand what we're dealing with," the Doctor said, his voice barely above a whisper, eyes fixed on the swirling mass of light and shadow. "This... is more than just a source of power. It's... alive."

"ENERGY SIGNATURES... INCONSISTENT WITH... KNOWN ENTITIES," one of the Cybermen intoned, its gaze locked on the vortex. "POTENTIAL... THREAT LEVEL... UNDETERMINED."

"Of course it is," the Doctor muttered, raising his sonic screwdriver to scan the vortex. The device whirred and clicked as it processed the data, its tip glowing a bright blue. "It's not just raw power," he continued, his voice gaining a hint of excitement. "It's a nexus point, a conduit between this world and... something else."

Kelnar stepped forward, his eyes wide with fear and wonder. "The Heart of Shadows," he whispered. "The legends say that it is the lifeblood of the world, the source from which the Death Moth draws its power."

"Not just its power," the Doctor corrected, his eyes narrowing as he studied the energy patterns within the vortex. "It's... its purpose. Look at this." He gestured to the symbols on the walls around the chamber.

"These carvings tell a story of cycles—destruction followed by regeneration. Life grows, expands, becomes chaotic... and then something must reset it. That's the Death Moth's role."

"DESTRUCTION OF... CYBER-KIND... CONFIRMED," the lead Cyberman stated, its voice harsh and mechanical. "THE ENTITY... SEEKS TO RESET... THE BALANCE."

"Yes, yes," the Doctor replied impatiently, waving his hand dismissively. "But it's not just destruction for its own sake." His eyes gleamed with realization as he turned to face the vortex. "It's a force of regeneration as well. It wipes out what disrupts the balance, but it also provides the means for life to start over. A clean slate, if you will."

Kelnar shook his head, his expression grim. "A clean slate at the cost of everything that exists? How can that be justified?"

The Doctor looked at him, his gaze serious. "It's not about justification, Kelnar. It's about the natural order, about the universe's way of correcting itself when things go too far out of balance. The Death Moth is like a cosmic gardener, pruning away the overgrowth to make way for new life. It's ruthless, yes, but it's not evil. It's... necessary."

"AND YET... IT THREATENS ALL," the Cyberman interjected. "CYBERMEN... WILL NOT BE ERASED."

"Of course not," the Doctor replied sharply, turning on the Cyberman. "You'd rather convert or destroy everything that doesn't fit into your vision of 'perfection.' But that's exactly the problem. You, the Daleks, you push the natural order to its breaking point. And when that happens, forces like the Death Moth are summoned to reset things."

He turned back to the vortex, his expression contemplative. "But what if," he murmured, almost to himself, "we could use that power for something other than destruction?"

Kelnar and the Cybermen remained silent, the air around them growing thick with tension. The Doctor's mind raced, connecting fragments of what he had learned. The Death Moth didn't just destroy—it created the conditions for something new to grow. It held the potential to regenerate, to restore what had been lost.

"The power of the Death Moth," the Doctor began, pacing in front of the vortex, "isn't just about wiping the slate clean. It's also about planting the seeds of new life. The legends here talk about worlds being reborn after the moth's passing, of civilizations rising anew from the ashes. The key isn't just in what it destroys, but in what it leaves behind."

"REGENERATION... OF LIFE?" the Cyberman questioned, its head tilting slightly. "EXPLAIN."

The Doctor stopped pacing and looked directly at the Cybermen. "Imagine," he said, his voice filled with intensity, "the worlds you and the Daleks have devastated. Planets stripped of life, cultures erased, ecosystems turned to dust. The Death Moth has the power to restore those worlds. It can accelerate the natural process of rebirth, creating the conditions for life to flourish once more."

"Then... it can heal our world?" Kelnar asked, hope flickering in his eyes.

The Doctor's gaze softened. "Yes, it can," he replied gently. "But at a cost. To do so, the Death Moth requires a sacrifice. Not just any sacrifice, but a total reset—a cleansing of all that currently exists on this world. It must burn away the chaos and imbalance to make way for new life."

"A RESET... IS UNACCEPTABLE," the Cyberman stated flatly. "CYBERMEN... WILL NOT BE ERASED."

"Yes, yes, you keep saying that," the Doctor snapped, his frustration bubbling to the surface. "But don't you see? This isn't about what you want or even what I want. It's about what the universe needs. The Death Moth doesn't act out of malice; it acts out of necessity."

Kelnar stepped forward, his expression torn. "You're saying that if we allow the Death Moth to complete its task, our world will be destroyed, but in time... it will be reborn?"

"Exactly," the Doctor replied, nodding. "The cost is great—everything you know, everyone you care about, gone in an instant. But in return, the world will be cleansed, and life will have a chance to start anew, free of the chaos and corruption that brought it to the brink."

Kelnar's face paled, his eyes searching the Doctor's for any hint of an alternative. "But... is there no other way?"

The Doctor hesitated, running a hand through his hair. "Maybe," he said slowly, his voice tinged with uncertainty. "The Death Moth is bound by its code, yes, but codes can be rewritten, paths can be altered. If we can show it that this world can find balance without a complete reset, we might be able to divert its course."

"DATA... SUPPORTS... POSSIBILITY," the Cyberman added, its voice quieter than usual. "IF... BALANCE IS RESTORED... THE ENTITY'S DIRECTIVE... MAY CHANGE."

"Exactly," the Doctor agreed, his eyes lighting up with determination. "We need to convince the Death Moth that this world is already on a path to regeneration. We have to show it that the Daleks and Cybermen are gone, that the cycle of destruction has ended. Only then might it leave, allowing life to continue without the need for a reset."

"But how?" Kelnar asked, his voice filled with desperation. "How can we possibly communicate that to such a force?"

The Doctor smiled faintly, raising his sonic screwdriver. "Through this," he said. "The Heart of Shadows is more than just a power source—it's a bridge, a conduit between the Death Moth and the universe. If I can modify the energy within this vortex, I can send a signal, a kind of... message, to the Death Moth. One that shows it that the balance can be achieved here, without the need for total destruction."

"RISK... HIGH," the Cyberman warned. "ENTITY MAY... INTERPRET SIGNAL AS... DECEPTION."

"Yes, it might," the Doctor admitted, his expression serious. "But it's the only chance we've got. If we do nothing, the Death Moth will cleanse this world in a wave of destruction, wiping out everything to start over. If we try to fight it, we'll be obliterated. This is the only path forward where there's even a sliver of hope."

Kelnar took a deep breath, nodding slowly. "Then we must try," he said quietly. "For the sake of our world, we must try."

The Doctor turned back to the vortex, his expression steely with resolve. "Alright then," he muttered, raising his sonic screwdriver. "Let's rewrite the rules."

He began to manipulate the energy patterns within the vortex, the sonic screwdriver emitting a series of high-pitched whines as it interfaced with the swirling mass of light and shadow. The chamber pulsed with energy, the walls vibrating as the Doctor worked to craft his message to the Death Moth.

"Come on," he muttered, his eyes fixed on the vortex. "Listen to me. This world doesn't need a reset; it just needs a chance."

The energy within the vortex began to shift, the light growing brighter and more focused. The Doctor could feel the power building, a resonance that echoed through the chamber like a heartbeat. It was working. The message was taking shape.

But then, the ground trembled violently, and a deafening hum filled the air. The Doctor staggered back, his eyes widening as the vortex flared with blinding light.

"No!" he shouted, shielding his face. "It's reacting!"

The chamber was filled with a deafening roar, and from the vortex emerged a burst of darkness, swirling and expanding until it coalesced into the form of the Death Moth. Its wings stretched wide, glowing with an ethereal light that filled the room with a cold, terrible beauty.

"You... heard me," the Doctor muttered, lowering his arm to stare at the creature before him. "Now, let's see if you'll listen."

The Death Moth hovered above the vortex, its eyes blazing with an intensity that bore into the Doctor's soul. *"Balance... must be... restored,"* it intoned, its voice echoing through the chamber.

"Yes," the Doctor replied, his voice steady despite the fear coursing through him. "But not through destruction. Look around you. The Daleks are gone, the Cybermen are beaten. This world is ready to heal, to find its own balance without being wiped clean."

The Death Moth remained silent, its wings beating slowly as it hovered in place. The Doctor held his breath, the tension in the air almost unbearable.

"Regeneration... requires... sacrifice," the Death Moth finally said, its voice cold and unwavering. *"Without sacrifice... balance... is... an illusion."*

The Doctor clenched his fists, his eyes blazing with determination. "Then let us be that sacrifice," he declared. "Take the remnants of what threatens this world—the machines, the twisted metal. Let them be the price for balance. But spare the life that still breathes, that still hopes."

The Death Moth's eyes flickered, its form shifting as it considered his words. For a moment, the Doctor sensed a hesitation, a hint of understanding.

"Come on," he whispered. "Please..."

The Death Moth began to glow, its wings folding around its body as it descended toward the vortex. The chamber filled with light, blinding and brilliant. The Doctor shielded his eyes, his heart pounding as he waited, hoping against hope that his plea had been heard.

Then, the light faded, and the Death Moth vanished into the vortex. The chamber grew still, the air heavy with silence. The Doctor lowered his arm, blinking as he looked around.

"It... left," Kelnar said, his voice trembling. "But... what does that mean?"

The Doctor exhaled slowly, a small, hopeful smile forming on his lips. "It means," he said quietly, "that we've been given a chance. The Death Moth has retreated, for now. Balance can be restored, but it's up to us to keep it that way."

He turned to the Cybermen, his expression hardening. "That means no more conversions, no more 'upgrading' life to fit your mold. This world will find its own path, free of interference."

The lead Cyberman tilted its head, its eyepiece glowing faintly. "UNDERSTOOD," it replied. "TEMPORARY... ALLIANCE... ENDED."

"Right," the Doctor said, turning back to the vortex. "Now, we have work to do. We have to help this world rebuild, to show the Death Moth that its trust in us wasn't misplaced."

And so, in the heart of the shadow world, the Doctor had uncovered the true power of the Death Moth—not just as a force of destruction, but as a harbinger of regeneration. The cost of its power was steep, but with the right balance and understanding, there was hope for new life to flourish. And the Doctor was determined to see that hope realized, no matter the cost.

Chapter 8: Daleks vs. Cybermen

The darkness of the shadow world was thick with tension, and the air itself felt charged, crackling with an eerie energy that signaled something was about to break loose. In the ruins of the ancient city, the Doctor stood with Kelnar beside him, the wind whipping at their clothes. In the distance, the Doctor could hear the mechanical whirring of the Cybermen and the rhythmic, metallic chanting of the Daleks. It wasn't hard to discern what was happening.

"Doctor, they're coming," Kelnar said, his voice tight with fear. "The Cybermen and the Daleks... both of them. They're heading toward each other."

"Of course they are," the Doctor muttered, his gaze fixed on the horizon where the dim glow of Dalek energy weapons was beginning to appear. "They can't help themselves, can they? Two unstoppable forces, each trying to prove they're the ultimate power in the universe. It's a miracle they haven't torn reality apart before now."

He turned to Kelnar, his eyes blazing with determination. "Get to safety. This is about to get very, very messy."

Kelnar hesitated, looking at the Doctor with wide, fearful eyes. "But what about you?"

The Doctor flashed a grim smile. "Oh, don't worry about me. I've been in the middle of more Dalek-Cybermen squabbles than I care to count. Just go. I'll try to keep them from destroying each other—and everything else in the process."

Kelnar nodded and hurried off into the shadows, leaving the Doctor standing alone in the ruins. He took a deep breath, pulling his coat tighter around him as he watched the inevitable collision course unfold.

The first sounds of battle reached him moments later. The Daleks advanced with their typical militaristic precision, their eyestalks swiveling and their gunsticks charged. On the other side, the Cybermen approached in their slow, methodical way, their weapons glinting in the dim light. The air was filled with the buzzing of Cyberman scanners and the rising chant of the Daleks.

"EXTERMINATE! EXTERMINATE!" the Daleks screeched in unison as they locked onto the approaching Cybermen.

"DELETE! DELETE!" the Cybermen responded, raising their arm-mounted weapons in a chilling show of force.

Then, all at once, chaos erupted.

The Daleks fired first, streams of blue energy lancing through the air toward the Cybermen. The Cybermen retaliated, sending beams of crackling energy straight back at their metal-clad enemies. Explosions rocked the ground as the energy blasts collided, sending showers of sparks and debris flying in every direction.

The Doctor ducked behind a crumbling stone pillar, wincing as a blast of heat seared the air above him. "Oh, wonderful," he muttered, peering out from behind his cover. "The universe's most notorious squabblers at it again. And here I am, stuck in the middle."

"CYBERMEN WILL BE DELETED!" a Dalek shrieked, its voice rising in pitch as it advanced, firing relentlessly.

"RESISTANCE IS FUTILE!" a Cyberman droned, its voice cold and emotionless as it unleashed another volley of energy toward the Daleks.

The battle intensified, with Daleks and Cybermen clashing in a brutal display of raw power and destruction. The ground shook beneath the relentless barrage of weapons, and the air filled with the acrid scent of burning metal. The Doctor could hear the whir of servos and the screech of tearing metal as Cybermen fell under the Dalek onslaught, only for more Cybermen to take their place.

"This is madness," the Doctor whispered, his eyes darting across the battlefield. "They're going to tear this world apart if they keep this up."

But even as he spoke, he could feel it—the change in the air. The temperature dropped suddenly, and a faint buzzing sound filled his ears, growing louder with every passing second. He knew what was coming.

"No," he murmured, his hearts skipping a beat. "Not now. Not like this."

From the shadows above, a faint glow began to appear, expanding and swirling as the air around it grew colder and heavier. The buzzing intensified, becoming a deep, resonant hum that sent shivers down the Doctor's spine.

The Death Moth had arrived.

The Doctor stepped out from behind the pillar, his eyes fixed on the glowing form descending from the sky. Its wings stretched wide, shimmering with an ethereal light that cast long, eerie shadows across the battlefield. The Daleks and Cybermen halted their assault, their attention drawn to the new presence that loomed above them.

"UNKNOWN ENTITY DETECTED!" a Dalek screamed, its eyestalk swiveling wildly. "INITIATE EXTERMINATION PROTOCOL!"

"ENTITY IS... NON-COMPLIANT!" a Cyberman intoned, raising its arm-mounted blaster. "PREPARE TO DELETE!"

"Stop!" the Doctor shouted, stepping forward with his arms raised. "Don't you see what's happening? You're disrupting the natural order, and the Death Moth is here to correct it!"

But his words were lost in the din of war cries. The Daleks fired first, streams of blue energy lancing toward the Death Moth. The Cybermen followed suit, unleashing beams of crackling power toward the glowing figure.

The Death Moth moved, its wings beating once. A shockwave of dark energy erupted from its form, crashing into the Dalek and Cyberman ranks. The Doctor staggered back, his coat flapping in the sudden gust of wind as the ground trembled beneath his feet.

The shockwave hit the Cybermen first, their metal casings buckling and twisting under the immense force. Sparks flew as their circuitry was overloaded, their limbs snapping off and clattering to the ground. The Daleks, too, were caught in the wave of destruction, their shells crumpling inward as if crushed by an invisible fist. Screeches of "EXTERMINATE!" and "DELETE!" filled the air, quickly turning into distorted howls as their voices were drowned out by the raw power of the Death Moth.

The Doctor watched, his hearts pounding, as the Death Moth unleashed its full fury. It descended upon the battlefield, sweeping its wings in a cataclysmic display of energy that sent shockwaves rippling through the ground. The Daleks and Cybermen were torn apart, their remains scattering like leaves in a hurricane. Metal fragments flew through the air, the last vestiges of their once-mighty forms.

"No, no, no!" the Doctor shouted, running forward, his sonic screwdriver buzzing frantically in his hand. "This isn't how it's supposed to go!"

But there was nothing he could do. The Death Moth hovered above the ruins of the battlefield, its eyes glowing with a cold, impersonal light. It was neither triumphant nor vengeful; it was simply acting in accordance with its purpose.

The Dalek Commander, battered and sparking, managed to raise its gunstick one last time. "YOU... WILL... BE... EXTERM—"

Its words were cut off as the Death Moth beat its wings again, and the Dalek's shell collapsed in on itself, crushed into a mass of twisted metal. Silence fell over the battlefield as the last echoes of the battle faded into the darkness.

The Doctor stood there, breathing heavily, his eyes locked on the Death Moth. It had wiped out both the Dalek and Cyberman forces in a matter of minutes, an overwhelming display of power that left no doubt as to its capabilities. It had not merely destroyed them; it had obliterated them, erasing their presence from the world in a surge of catastrophic energy.

"Why?" the Doctor whispered, his voice trembling with a mix of anger and sorrow. "Why did it have to end this way?"

The Death Moth turned its gaze toward him, its eyes glowing with an intensity that sent chills down his spine. It was not malevolent, nor was it remorseful. It simply was—a force of balance acting in accordance with the cosmic order.

"Disruption... eradicated," it intoned, its voice echoing through the air like a haunting whisper. *"Balance... restored."*

The Doctor shook his head, his eyes blazing with defiance. "You don't have to do this!" he shouted. "There's another way! You don't have to destroy everything to restore balance!"

The Death Moth hovered silently for a moment, its form flickering like a candle in the wind. Then, slowly, it began to ascend, its wings folding around its body as it rose into the darkness of the sky. The buzzing hum faded, leaving behind an eerie stillness that settled over the battlefield.

The Doctor fell to his knees, his eyes staring at the wreckage around him. Daleks and Cybermen lay in heaps, their remains twisted and broken beyond recognition. The ground was scorched and pitted, the air heavy with the scent of burning metal.

"It didn't have to be like this," he murmured, his voice choked with grief and frustration. "You didn't have to die... any of you."

Kelnar emerged from the shadows, his face pale as he took in the scene before him. "Doctor," he said quietly, kneeling beside him. "Is it over?"

The Doctor took a deep breath, his gaze fixed on the sky where the Death Moth had disappeared. "For now," he replied, his voice hollow. "But this is far from the end. The Death Moth will continue to act according to its nature, wiping out whatever it deems a threat to the balance."

Kelnar looked at him, his eyes filled with fear. "Then what can we do?"

The Doctor slowly rose to his feet, his face set with grim resolve. "We learn," he said firmly. "We understand its purpose, its rules. And we find a way to show it that balance can be achieved without destruction."

He turned and began walking away from the battlefield, his coat billowing out behind him. "But first," he added, glancing over his shoulder at Kelnar, "we have to make sure this world is ready to change. Because if it isn't... the Death Moth will return."

And so, as the shadow world lay silent once more, the Doctor set off on his path. The battle between the Daleks and Cybermen had only confirmed what he already knew: the Death Moth was a force that would not be swayed by mere words. It acted with a singular purpose, one that the Doctor was determined to understand and, if possible, redirect.

The universe demanded balance, but at what cost? That was the question the Doctor now carried with him as he ventured into the unknown, ready to confront the nature of the Death Moth and the cosmic order it sought to uphold.

Chapter 9: The Doctor's Dilemma

The shadow world had grown eerily quiet in the aftermath of the battle. The ground was still scorched and scattered with the remains of Daleks and Cybermen. The acrid scent of burnt metal hung heavily in the air, a grim reminder of the Death Moth's catastrophic power. The Doctor stood alone amidst the ruins, his mind a storm of conflicting thoughts and emotions.

He turned slowly, his eyes scanning the horizon. The Death Moth had vanished into the sky after wiping out the two armies, leaving behind an unsettling calm. In that silence, the Doctor could feel the weight of his responsibility pressing down on him. The Death Moth wasn't just a mindless force of destruction; it was an enforcer of balance. Yet, its method of achieving that balance was ruthless, indifferent to the suffering it caused.

"What do I do now?" he muttered to himself, running a hand through his hair. "This thing—this force—it's beyond anything I've encountered before. It's not evil, but it's not good either. It just... is."

Kelnar approached him from behind, his footsteps cautious on the cracked earth. "Doctor?" he said hesitantly. "What happens now? The Death Moth... it's gone, but for how long?"

The Doctor didn't answer immediately. He walked a few paces forward, his eyes locked on the horizon where the moth had disappeared. "That's the problem, isn't it?" he finally replied, his voice tinged with frustration. "It's gone, yes. But it's not defeated. It's never really gone. The Death Moth is part of the universe's way of keeping things in check. And that's the dilemma."

Kelnar furrowed his brow. "What do you mean?"

The Doctor turned to face him, his expression serious. "I mean that this creature is far too powerful for anyone to control. Not the Daleks, not the Cybermen, not even me. It acts according to its purpose—restoring balance by erasing what it deems an imbalance. But who decides what that imbalance is? The moth? The universe? And if I try to interfere, who am I to dictate what balance should be?"

Kelnar remained silent, his face pale as he absorbed the Doctor's words. "So what do we do?" he asked quietly. "If it returns, it will destroy us all, won't it?"

The Doctor sighed, turning away again. "That's just it. If I try to destroy it, I become the very thing it seeks to correct: a force disrupting the natural order. But if I let it continue unchecked, it could wipe out entire civilizations in its quest for balance. I'm stuck between action and inaction, and both come at a terrible cost."

He began to pace, his mind whirling with possibilities. "I could try to trap it," he muttered, more to himself than to Kelnar. "But then, it becomes a prisoner, a tool to be wielded. That's not balance; that's control. And using it for good? To restore worlds? That's a gamble. Who's to say I wouldn't become like the Daleks or the Cybermen, deciding which worlds get to live and which must perish?"

Kelnar watched him, his expression a mixture of fear and hope. "You're the Doctor," he said slowly. "You always find a way. Maybe there's something we haven't thought of yet?"

The Doctor stopped pacing, his eyes narrowing as he turned to Kelnar. "Oh, I always find a way, don't I?" he replied bitterly. "The question is, which way is the right one? I've talked down gods, stopped invasions, rewritten the rules of time itself. But this? This is different. The Death Moth is a cosmic constant, a part of the fabric of reality. To destroy it would be to unravel a piece of the universe itself."

Kelnar stepped closer, his voice trembling. "But isn't that why you're here? To make the hard choices? If anyone can find a way to reason with this creature, to change its purpose, it's you."

The Doctor stared at him, his eyes intense. "And if I fail?" he asked quietly. "If I try to reason with it and it refuses to change, then what? Do I let it continue its rampage? Do I allow entire worlds to be erased in the name of balance?"

Kelnar looked down, struggling for words. "I... I don't know," he admitted. "But you can't just do nothing."

"No," the Doctor agreed, his voice grim. "I can't. But I can't just do something reckless, either. That's how wars start, how civilizations fall. One misstep, and I could end up causing more harm than the Death Moth ever could."

He turned his back on Kelnar, staring out at the horizon again. "I've faced beings of unimaginable power before," he said softly, almost as if speaking to the wind. "But they were individuals—conscious entities with motives, desires, egos. The Death Moth is different. It's like a natural disaster, a cosmic storm with a purpose. It doesn't want to kill; it simply does because that's how it maintains the universe's balance."

Kelnar took a cautious step forward. "So... what's your plan, Doctor?"

The Doctor didn't answer immediately. He closed his eyes, feeling the cold wind on his face, the faint hum of the universe around him. He needed a plan, but every option carried a risk that weighed heavily on his shoulders.

"If I destroy it," he said finally, opening his eyes, "I risk throwing the universe into chaos. The balance it seeks to uphold would be lost, and who knows what kind of power vacuum would emerge? But if I let it continue unchecked..."

He trailed off, his mind racing. He had always been the one to stand against tyrants, to defy cosmic forces that sought to impose their will on the universe. But now, he was facing a force that didn't impose—it simply corrected. How could he, in good conscience, destroy something that was merely fulfilling its role in the natural order?

"No," he murmured, shaking his head. "I can't destroy it. Not yet, not without trying everything else first."

Kelnar blinked, a flicker of hope in his eyes. "Then what will you do?"

The Doctor turned to face him, his expression fierce. "I'm going to talk to it," he declared. "I'm going to find a way to reason with it, to make it see that there are other ways to restore balance than through destruction. It's sentient—somewhere inside that mass of energy and purpose is a mind that can be reached. I have to believe that."

Kelnar's eyes widened. "But how? You've already tried speaking to it, and it nearly wiped us out!"

"Yes," the Doctor acknowledged, nodding. "But that was on its terms. It came to us as a force of judgment. This time, I need to approach it from a place of understanding, to enter its domain willingly. I need to show it that I'm not here to stop it but to find a new way."

He began walking toward the ancient temple ruins, his pace quick and determined. "I'll use the Heart of Shadows again, but not to send a signal. This time, I'll use it as a doorway, a bridge into the Death Moth's consciousness. If I can make it see the potential for balance through regeneration without the need for destruction..."

"Then you think it will change its ways?" Kelnar asked, hurrying to keep up.

"I don't know," the Doctor replied, his tone hard and resolute. "But I have to try. Because if I don't, the only option left is to destroy it. And I will, if that's what it comes to. But only as a last resort."

They reached the entrance to the temple, and the Doctor stopped, turning to Kelnar. "This is where we part ways," he said gently. "I need you to stay out here. If things go wrong... well, someone has to survive to tell the tale."

Kelnar nodded, his face pale but determined. "I understand. Good luck, Doctor."

The Doctor managed a small, bittersweet smile. "Luck, Kelnar, has nothing to do with it. It's all about timing, words, and a bit of hope." With that, he turned and entered the temple, the darkness swallowing him as he descended toward the Heart of Shadows.

As he reached the chamber, the familiar hum of the vortex filled his ears. He approached the swirling mass of energy, raising his sonic screwdriver. "Alright, you cosmic force of balance," he muttered, his eyes locked on the vortex. "Time to have a proper conversation."

He activated the screwdriver, sending a pulse of energy into the vortex. The room filled with light, and the air grew cold, the shadows around him deepening. Slowly, the glow coalesced into a familiar form—the Death Moth, its wings stretching wide, casting a ghostly light across the chamber.

"You... return," it intoned, its voice echoing through the air. *"Purpose... must be... fulfilled."*

The Doctor took a deep breath, stepping forward. "I'm not here to stop you," he said calmly, his voice firm but gentle. "I'm here to understand you. To find another way to achieve balance without destroying everything in your path."

The Death Moth's eyes glowed, its form rippling as if caught in a struggle. *"Balance... requires... correction. Imbalance... cannot... persist."*

"Yes, I know," the Doctor replied, his gaze unwavering. "But correction doesn't have to mean obliteration. It can mean guidance, nurturing, allowing things to grow in a new direction. You have the power to restore, not just destroy."

The Death Moth remained silent, its wings beating slowly. The Doctor felt its presence pressing into his mind, an ancient, cold consciousness that sought to understand his intentions.

"Listen to me," the Doctor continued, his voice rising with urgency. "You don't have to be a force of death. You can be a force of life, of renewal. The universe needs balance, yes, but balance can be achieved through growth, through harmony. Not just through erasure."

The air grew heavy, and the Doctor could feel the weight of the Death Moth's deliberation. It was considering his words, weighing them against its cosmic purpose.

"Balance... can... evolve," it finally said, its voice softer, almost contemplative.

The Doctor's hearts skipped a beat. "Yes!" he exclaimed, stepping closer. "Balance can evolve. You can be the catalyst for that evolution. You can guide worlds, not just reset them."

The Death Moth hovered above the vortex, its form flickering. *"If... balance... evolves... cost... remains."*

The Doctor nodded, his face somber. "I know. Every action has a cost. But that cost doesn't have to be total destruction. It can be the hard work of change, of rebuilding. The choice, ultimately, is yours."

The room fell silent, the air crackling with the energy of the Death Moth's thoughts. The Doctor waited, his hearts pounding. This was it—the turning point.

Finally, the Death Moth began to ascend, its wings folding around its body. *"Balance... will... change,"* it intoned, its voice echoing through the chamber. *"But the cost... must be... accepted."*

The Doctor nodded, his eyes fierce. "We will pay it, whatever it is. Because that's what life is—struggle, sacrifice, and hope."

The Death Moth vanished into the vortex, and the chamber grew quiet. The Doctor stood there, breathing heavily, the enormity of what had just happened washing over him.

He had done it. He had found another way.

But the cost... that was a question yet to be answered.

Chapter 10: The Dalek Trap

The shadow world lay in a deceptive calm as the Doctor emerged from the temple. The encounter with the Death Moth had left him shaken, but also determined. For a brief moment, he had reached the cosmic entity, shown it that balance could be achieved without mass destruction. But he knew the struggle wasn't over; the Death Moth's evolution hinged on a fragile promise of change, and the cost had yet to reveal itself.

Kelnar approached cautiously, eyes filled with apprehension. "Doctor, what happened in there? Did you... reach it?"

"Yes," the Doctor replied, his voice steady but tinged with fatigue. "I got through to it, just barely. It's willing to change, to explore a new way of restoring balance. But it came with a warning—a cost that we may not be prepared to pay."

Kelnar nodded slowly, a glimmer of hope in his eyes. "Then there's still a chance?"

"There is," the Doctor confirmed, his eyes scanning the horizon warily. "But not if others interfere."

As if on cue, a faint whirring sound echoed from the distance, growing louder with every second. The Doctor's expression darkened. "Speaking of interference..."

From the shadows, the Daleks began to appear, their metallic forms glinting ominously in the dim light. They moved in perfect formation, gliding toward the Doctor and Kelnar with a predatory grace. The Doctor's jaw tightened as he took in their presence.

"Ah, Daleks," he muttered under his breath, his eyes narrowing. "I should have known you wouldn't stay out of this for long."

"DOCTOR!" a Dalek shrieked, its eyestalk swiveling toward him. "YOU WILL SURRENDER IMMEDIATELY!"

The Doctor straightened, adjusting his coat and raising an eyebrow. "Really? We're going with the 'surrender' bit, are we? Seems a tad predictable, even for you."

The lead Dalek, marked with additional ridges and panels denoting its rank as a commander, glided forward. Its gunstick aimed directly at the Doctor, glowing faintly. "YOU WILL OBEY!" it screeched. "THE DEATH MOTH WILL BE CONTAINED, AND ITS POWER HARNESSSED FOR THE DALEK EMPIRE!"

The Doctor frowned, his eyes flicking toward the horizon, already guessing at their plan. "Oh, I see," he said, his tone darkening. "You've set a trap, haven't you? You're not just here to threaten me; you're here to force me into a choice."

"CORRECT!" the Dalek Commander responded, a hint of triumph in its harsh voice. "THE DEATH MOTH HAS BEEN LURED INTO OUR DESIGNATED CONTAINMENT ZONE. IF YOU ATTEMPT TO SAVE IT, YOU WILL BE DESTROYED. IF YOU DO NOT, THE ENTITY WILL BE OBLITERATED!"

The Doctor's hearts skipped a beat. His mind raced as he processed the situation. The Daleks had somehow managed to lure the Death Moth into a trap—probably using the residual energy from their previous battle as bait. Now they were trying to force his hand, hoping to make him either kill the moth or sacrifice himself in an attempt to save it.

"So that's your game," he said slowly, a grim look settling on his face. "You think you can force me to choose between letting you take control of a cosmic force or destroying it myself."

"YOU HAVE NO OTHER OPTIONS!" the Dalek shrieked. "OBEY, OR BE EXTERMINATED!"

Kelnar took a step back, his face pale with fear. "Doctor, what are we going to do?" he whispered, his eyes darting between the Doctor and the advancing Daleks.

The Doctor remained silent for a moment, his mind whirling. There had to be a way out of this. He knew the Death Moth was too powerful for the Daleks to contain for long, but if he did nothing, they would provoke it into unleashing its full destructive potential. On the other hand, attacking the Daleks head-on would likely result in the moth being pushed into a rampage.

"Think, think, think," he muttered under his breath, his gaze flicking to the darkened sky. He had one chance to turn this situation to his advantage, and it was going to require a delicate touch.

He turned to Kelnar, his eyes sharp. "When I say run, run back to the temple and use the carvings to connect with the Heart of Shadows. It's the only way to communicate with the Death Moth and tell it to hold off its attack."

Kelnar blinked in confusion. "But how will you...?"

"No time to explain!" the Doctor cut him off, raising his voice so the Daleks could hear. "You lot!" he shouted, turning toward the Daleks. "You've forgotten something very important about the Death Moth."

The Dalek Commander hesitated, its eyestalk swiveling toward the Doctor. "EXPLAIN!" it demanded.

The Doctor took a slow, deliberate step forward. "The Death Moth isn't just a force of destruction," he began, his voice carrying across the ruins. "It's a force of regeneration, bound by a cosmic code to restore balance. You can't control it, no matter how much you try. If you push it, you'll only provoke it into wiping you out."

"LIES!" the Dalek shrieked. "THE DEATH MOTH IS POWER! DALEKS WILL HARNESS ITS POWER TO EXTERMINATE ALL LIFE FORMS!"

"Right," the Doctor muttered under his breath. "Stubborn as ever, aren't you?" He took a deep breath and raised his sonic screwdriver, pointing it toward the ground. "Well then, you leave me no choice."

"EXTERMINATE!" the Dalek screamed, firing its weapon.

The Doctor dived to the side, rolling across the rubble as the energy blast struck the ground where he had stood. He sprang to his feet, twisting the sonic screwdriver and aiming it at the sky. A high-pitched whine filled the air, and the ground trembled.

"RUN!" the Doctor shouted to Kelnar.

Kelnar didn't hesitate. He turned and sprinted toward the temple, his footsteps echoing through the ruins. The Daleks fired after him, but the Doctor waved his screwdriver, releasing a burst of energy that disrupted their aim.

"YOU WILL NOT ESCAPE!" the Dalek Commander screeched, swiveling its eyestalk back to the Doctor.

The Doctor stood his ground, his eyes fixed on the sky above. "You're not listening!" he shouted. "The Death Moth is bound to this world. You can't trap it, you can't contain it. And if you try, it will destroy everything!"

A low hum filled the air, growing louder and more intense. The Doctor felt the temperature drop, a sure sign that the Death Moth was responding. He glanced toward the horizon and saw it—a faint glow that expanded into a swirling storm of light and shadow.

"Too late," he murmured, his eyes narrowing. "You've provoked it."

The Death Moth appeared in the sky, its wings stretching wide, casting a ghostly light across the battlefield. The Daleks froze, their eyestalks swiveling toward the creature as it descended, its presence filling the air with a sense of impending doom.

"EXTERMINATE!" the Dalek Commander screamed, firing its weapon.

The Death Moth moved, its wings beating once with a cataclysmic force. A shockwave of dark energy erupted from its form, sweeping across the battlefield. The ground shook violently as the energy wave crashed into the Dalek ranks. Metal screeched and twisted as the Daleks' casings crumpled inward, their screams of "EXTERMINATE!" turning into distorted, dying echoes.

The Doctor shielded his face from the blast, his hearts pounding. "No, no, no," he muttered. "This wasn't supposed to happen!"

But even as the Daleks were obliterated, the Death Moth continued its advance. The Doctor could feel its attention turning toward him, its eyes glowing with an intense, inscrutable light. It had sensed the imbalance—the threat posed by the Daleks—and now it sought to correct it.

He raised his sonic screwdriver, sending a pulse of energy into the sky. "I know you can hear me!" he shouted. "This isn't the way! I'm trying to help you restore balance, not destroy it!"

The air around him crackled with energy, and the Death Moth paused, hovering above the ruins. Its wings beat slowly, casting swirling shadows across the ground. For a moment, the Doctor felt the weight of its presence pressing into his mind—a vast, cold consciousness that sought to understand his intent.

"Listen to me," he continued, his voice strained but firm. "The Daleks are gone. You don't need to continue this cycle of destruction. There are other ways to restore balance, to regenerate what was lost."

A flicker of light passed through the Death Moth's form, and the air grew still. The Doctor held his breath, his mind racing. Was it listening? Was there still a chance?

From the direction of the temple, a faint glow appeared, growing brighter as Kelnar emerged, his face bathed in the light of the Heart of Shadows. He held up his hands, and the energy surrounding him resonated with the hum of the vortex.

"The Heart of Shadows," the Doctor murmured, his eyes widening. "It's... responding."

The Death Moth turned, its attention shifting toward the temple and the glow emanating from Kelnar. For a moment, the air was filled with an overwhelming silence. Then, the moth's wings beat again, this time sending a wave of light toward the Heart of Shadows.

The Doctor watched, his hearts in his throat, as the energy from the moth merged with the light of the Heart, creating a swirling mass of light and shadow. Slowly, the Death Moth began to ascend, its form dissolving into the vortex of energy.

"It's... leaving," Kelnar said, his voice trembling with awe.

The Doctor let out a breath he hadn't realized he'd been holding. "Not leaving," he corrected. "It's returning to the heart of this world, where it belongs. The Dalek trap forced its hand, but we showed it there's another way."

He turned to Kelnar, a faint smile playing on his lips. "We did it."

Kelnar nodded, his face pale but hopeful. "For now. But what if it returns?"

The Doctor's expression grew somber. "It will, one day. The Death Moth is part of the universe's cycle. But next time, we'll be ready. We'll have learned how to live in balance, how to coexist without tipping the scales into chaos."

As the light of the Heart of Shadows faded, the Doctor lowered his sonic screwdriver, feeling the tension in the air dissipate. The Death Moth had returned to its place, the balance temporarily restored. But the journey was far from over.

He turned to Kelnar, a look of determination in his eyes. "Now, we start rebuilding. We prove to the universe—and to the Death Moth—that balance can be achieved without more death."

Kelnar nodded, a flicker of resolve crossing his face. "We will. Together."

The Doctor looked out over the ruins, the remnants of the Dalek trap scattered around them. "Yes," he said quietly. "Together."

The trap had failed. The Daleks' plan to force his hand had been thwarted, but the Doctor knew that this victory was only a small part of a larger struggle. The Death Moth had shown him that balance was not about power or control, but about harmony. And now, it was up to him to ensure that harmony was maintained, even in a universe that seemed determined to disrupt it.

Chapter 11: The Cybermen's Gamble

The ruins of the shadow world were eerily quiet after the confrontation with the Daleks, but the Doctor could sense that this peace was only temporary. The Death Moth had returned to the heart of the world, a cosmic force temporarily quelled by his intervention. Yet, he knew that danger still lingered on the horizon. Not every threat had been extinguished, and he feared what might come next.

As if answering his thoughts, a faint mechanical whirring reached his ears. The Doctor turned sharply toward the source, his eyes narrowing. Through the mist that clung to the decaying city, he saw them—figures moving in the distance. The remnants of the Cybermen, their metal bodies reflecting the faint, ghostly light of the shadow world.

"Doctor," Kelnar whispered, stepping up beside him. "The Cybermen... they're still here?"

"Yes," the Doctor muttered, his expression grim. "They survived the last encounter, and they're not about to give up now. Especially not after seeing the Death Moth's power." He clenched his fists, a storm of thoughts racing through his mind. The Cybermen were relentless in their pursuit of 'perfection.' If they intended to merge their technology with the Death Moth's power, the consequences could be catastrophic.

"We need to stop them," he said, determination hardening his voice. "They're going to try and harness the Death Moth, to make themselves invincible. And that's going to end in disaster—for them and for this world."

Kelnar looked at him, fear flickering in his eyes. "But how? They'll never listen to reason."

The Doctor took a deep breath, steeling himself. "They won't listen to reason, no. But we have to try and intercept them before they provoke the Death Moth. If they succeed in even partially merging with its power, they could destabilize everything—the balance, the cycle, this world's very existence."

Without another word, the Doctor started toward the distant figures, his footsteps echoing softly against the cracked earth. Kelnar followed closely, his face a mask of grim resolve.

As they approached, the Cybermen came into full view. They were clustered in a circle, their heads tilted toward a central device—a large, cylindrical machine bristling with wires and conduits. The machine emitted a low hum, its surface etched with symbols reminiscent of the carvings inside the temple.

"Cybermen!" the Doctor called out, striding forward with his hands raised. "Step away from that device, now!"

The Cybermen turned in unison, their eyepieces glowing ominously in the dim light. The lead Cyberman, distinguished by additional armor plating and a series of symbols engraved across its chest, stepped forward.

"DOCTOR," it intoned, its voice a harsh, metallic rasp. "YOU WILL NOT INTERFERE. THE DEATH MOTH'S POWER WILL BE... ASSIMILATED."

The Doctor gritted his teeth, his eyes flashing with anger. "Assimilated? You think you can just plug into a force of cosmic balance and turn it into a power source? You don't understand what you're dealing with! The Death Moth isn't just energy—it's a consciousness, a force that obeys its own rules."

"INCORRECT," the Cyberman replied, its gaze fixed on the Doctor. "THE DEATH MOTH IS... ENERGY. IT WILL BE RECONFIGURED TO SERVE... THE CYBERMEN."

Kelnar's eyes widened with horror. "You're insane," he breathed. "You'll destroy yourselves and everything around you!"

The Cyberman turned its head slightly, its expression—or what passed for an expression—unreadable. "RISK... ACCEPTABLE. THE CYBERMEN WILL BECOME... INVINCIBLE."

The Doctor's eyes darted to the machine at the center of the Cybermen's formation. It was a conduit designed to tap into the Death Moth's energy, an array of technological components combined with elements from the shadow world's ancient technology. He realized what they were attempting: a forced merger, using the machine to interface directly with the moth's power source.

"Stop this now!" the Doctor shouted, his voice ringing through the ruins. "If you try to connect with the Death Moth, it will retaliate. It will see you as a threat to the balance and wipe you out."

"THE CYBERMEN WILL EVOLVE!" the lead Cyberman declared, raising its arm toward the machine. "THE DEATH MOTH WILL BE... ASSIMILATED."

With that, the Cyberman activated the device. The machine whirred to life, emitting a piercing, high-pitched hum. Beams of light shot out from its surface, converging into a single point above the Cybermen. The air grew cold, and the ground beneath their feet began to vibrate.

The Doctor felt a chill run down his spine. "No, no, no!" he muttered, clutching his sonic screwdriver. "They're forcing a connection. This is bad. This is very bad."

From the sky above, a swirl of darkness began to form, expanding outward like a storm. The Doctor's eyes widened as the familiar glow of the Death Moth appeared, its wings stretching out in a magnificent yet terrifying display of power. It descended toward the Cybermen, the air around it crackling with raw energy.

The Doctor stepped forward, waving his screwdriver in a desperate attempt to disrupt the machine's signal. "Stop this now!" he shouted. "You're provoking it! It's going to—"

But his warning came too late. The Death Moth hovered above the machine, its wings beating slowly. The light from the machine began to pulse, sending waves of energy toward the creature. For a brief moment, it seemed as though the Cybermen's gamble might succeed; the Death Moth's form flickered, its energy intertwining with the beams emanating from the device.

"INTERFACE... ESTABLISHED," the lead Cyberman intoned, its voice laced with a hollow triumph. "CYBERMEN WILL... EVOLVE."

The Doctor watched in horror as the machine's energy patterns changed, the swirling light around the Death Moth becoming erratic, unstable. "No," he whispered. "They're disrupting its essence. It's going to—"

Suddenly, the Death Moth's eyes blazed with an intense, blinding light. The air grew impossibly cold, and the ground shook violently. With a deafening roar, the creature unleashed a wave of pure, unbridled energy that surged outward, slamming into the Cybermen and their machine.

"WARNING! SYSTEMS OVERLOAD!" the lead Cyberman screamed, its voice warping as sparks erupted from its body. "ERROR... ERR—"

The blast hit the Cybermen with the force of a cataclysm. Their metallic casings crumpled inward, their circuits shorting out in bursts of light and sound. The machine at the center of their formation exploded, sending shards of metal and debris flying in every direction. The Cybermen were torn apart, their limbs scattered across the battlefield as the Death Moth's energy washed over them, leaving nothing but smoldering ruins in its wake.

The Doctor staggered back, shielding his eyes from the blinding light. The roar of energy filled his ears, drowning out every other sound. He felt the ground beneath him shake, the air itself vibrating with the force of the Death Moth's fury.

When the light finally faded, the Doctor lowered his arm, blinking in the sudden stillness. The Cybermen were gone. Where they had stood, only scorched earth and twisted fragments of metal remained. The machine was a smoldering wreck, its components melted and fused into a single, unrecognizable mass.

The Death Moth hovered above the ruins, its wings beating slowly, almost serenely. It had acted with the cold efficiency of a force of nature, eradicating the threat with an overwhelming display of power. There had been no hesitation, no mercy—only the ruthless correction of an imbalance.

The Doctor took a deep, shuddering breath. "You... did what you had to," he murmured, his voice barely audible in the silence. "They forced your hand. They tried to become something they were never meant to be."

The Death Moth turned its gaze toward him, its eyes glowing with a light that seemed to pierce through his very soul. For a moment, he felt the enormity of its presence—a consciousness ancient and vast, bound to the cosmic order it sought to uphold.

"BALANCE... RESTORED," it intoned, its voice echoing through the ruins like a whisper from the depths of time.

The Doctor nodded, his face grim. "Yes, balance restored... at a cost." He gestured to the wreckage around them. "You wiped them out. You had no choice, did you? They pushed too far."

The Death Moth remained silent, its form rippling as it hovered above the battlefield. The Doctor could feel its energy pulsating through the air, an ever-present reminder of its power and purpose.

"You're a force of balance," he continued, taking a step forward. "But balance isn't just about destruction. It's about guiding, evolving. The Cybermen failed to see that, and they paid the price. But not every world needs to end this way."

The Death Moth's wings beat slowly, casting swirling shadows across the ground. The Doctor watched it intently, searching for any sign of understanding. "Listen to me," he said, his voice steady. "There are other ways to correct the imbalance, ways that don't involve obliteration. It's not too late to change."

For a long, tense moment, the Death Moth hovered in place. The air around them grew still, as if the world itself were holding its breath. Then, slowly, the moth began to ascend, its wings folding around its body.

"EVOLUTION... REQUIRES... UNDERSTANDING," it intoned, its voice echoing softly through the ruins. "BALANCE... WILL... CHANGE."

The Doctor exhaled, his shoulders sagging with relief. "Yes," he murmured. "It will."

The Death Moth vanished into the sky, leaving behind a silence that settled over the battlefield. The Doctor stood there, staring at the spot where it had disappeared, his mind heavy with the weight of what had just transpired.

Kelnar approached cautiously, his eyes wide with awe and fear. "Doctor, is it... over?"

The Doctor shook his head slowly. "Not over," he replied. "Not by a long shot. But the Cybermen's gamble has failed, and the Death Moth has... learned something today. It's beginning to evolve, to see that balance can be more than just destruction."

He turned to face Kelnar, his eyes filled with determination. "But it's up to us now. We have to show the universe that balance can be achieved through growth, through harmony. Otherwise, the next time the Death Moth returns, there might not be anyone left to reason with it."

Kelnar nodded, his face set with resolve. "Then we'll do it, Doctor. We'll rebuild, and we'll find that balance."

The Doctor offered a small, weary smile. "Yes," he said quietly. "We will."

And so, amidst the ruins of the Cybermen's failed gamble, the Doctor stood ready to face the future. The Death Moth had unleashed its fury, but it had also shown a capacity to change, to evolve. The universe demanded balance, and the Doctor was determined to guide it toward a new understanding—a balance that embraced life rather than obliterated it.

Chapter 12: The Doctor's Escape

The shadow world's ruins lay eerily silent, a grim testament to the recent chaos. The Doctor had thought the worst was over after the Cybermen's demise, but the Daleks were not so easily deterred. As he and Kelnar navigated the crumbling remains of the ancient city, the Doctor sensed a creeping tension in the air. The Daleks were out there, plotting, and he knew it was only a matter of time before they made their next move.

"Kelnar," the Doctor began, his eyes scanning the horizon warily, "the Daleks won't stop until they've seized or destroyed the Death Moth. They're too driven by their thirst for power."

Kelnar glanced at him, his face pale. "But they saw what happened to the Cybermen. Surely, they know they can't control it?"

The Doctor shook his head, a bitter smile forming on his lips. "They know, but they don't care. The Daleks are arrogant. They believe that if they can't control it, then no one can. And that makes them incredibly dangerous."

They continued through the ruins, the oppressive silence broken only by the crunch of gravel beneath their feet. A chill wind swept through the city, carrying with it an unsettling sense of foreboding. The Doctor knew he needed to find a way to protect the Death Moth, to ensure that it could evolve and learn to maintain balance without resorting to obliteration. But how could he protect a force of nature from beings as ruthless as the Daleks?

Suddenly, a faint, rhythmic whirring filled the air. The Doctor froze, his hearts skipping a beat. He recognized that sound. "Oh no," he muttered, his eyes widening. "Kelnar, get back! It's a trap!"

Before Kelnar could react, the air was filled with the harsh, metallic voices of the Daleks. "DOCTOR! YOU ARE SURROUNDED! SURRENDER IMMEDIATELY!"

From the shadows, Daleks glided forward, their eyestalks swiveling toward the Doctor and Kelnar. A dozen of them emerged, forming a circle that cut off every possible escape route. The Doctor gritted his teeth, quickly scanning their formation. They had him cornered, and they knew it.

"Ah, Daleks," the Doctor said with forced nonchalance, raising his hands in mock surrender. "Surrounding me again? You do know this is starting to feel rather repetitive, don't you?"

"YOUR DEFIANCE IS FUTILE!" the lead Dalek barked, its voice grating with a hint of triumph. "YOU WILL BE EXTERMINATED IF YOU DO NOT COMPLY!"

The Doctor's eyes darted around, searching for any means of escape. The ruins offered little cover, and the Daleks had positioned themselves perfectly to block any route he might take. Trapped, with no TARDIS in sight and no sonic trick that could get him out of this one. "Alright, alright," he muttered to himself. "Think, Doctor. There has to be a way out of this."

Kelnar, standing just behind him, looked terrified. "Doctor, what are we going to do?" he whispered, his voice trembling.

The Doctor took a deep breath, his mind racing. "We're going to stall," he replied quietly. "I need time to think."

He turned back to the Daleks, forcing a smile. "So, what's the plan then, hmm? Exterminate me and risk the wrath of the Death Moth? Not the brightest idea, is it?"

The Dalek Commander moved forward, its eyestalk glowing as it locked onto the Doctor. "THE DEATH MOTH WILL BE... NEUTRALIZED," it declared coldly. "YOU WILL ASSIST OR BE DESTROYED."

"Neutralized? You can't neutralize a force of nature!" the Doctor retorted, anger flashing in his eyes. "The Death Moth isn't a weapon you can simply switch off or repurpose. If you try to control it, you'll provoke a reaction that could destroy you all!"

"IRRELEVANT!" the Dalek Commander screeched. "THE DOCTOR WILL OBEY! THE DEATH MOTH IS POWER! DALEKS WILL DOMINATE OR EXTERMINATE!"

The Doctor's jaw tightened. He was running out of options. He needed to break free, but how? As he glanced up at the darkened sky, a flicker of light caught his eye. His hearts skipped a beat as he recognized the faint glow of ethereal wings materializing in the distance.

The Death Moth was coming.

The Doctor felt a strange mix of relief and dread. He didn't know why, but the creature had shown a peculiar connection to him. Perhaps it sensed his intentions or recognized that he sought balance rather than chaos. Whatever the reason, it had spared him before, and he hoped it would do so again.

The Daleks, however, noticed the approaching entity as well. "WARNING!" one of them shrieked, swiveling its eyestalk toward the sky. "DEATH MOTH APPROACHING! INITIATE CONTAINMENT PROTOCOL!"

"No!" the Doctor shouted, stepping forward with urgency. "Don't do this! You'll only provoke it further!"

But the Daleks were not listening. They fired their weapons into the sky, streams of blue energy lancing toward the swirling form of the Death Moth. The air crackled with power, and the earth beneath them trembled.

The Death Moth descended with a roar of wind and shadow, its wings beating furiously as it hovered above the battlefield. The Daleks' energy blasts struck it, but they merely dissipated against its form, absorbed like water into a sponge. The Doctor watched in awe and terror as the creature's eyes glowed, its entire body pulsating with an unearthly light.

"YOU WILL BE EXTERMINATED!" the Daleks screamed, firing again.

The Death Moth moved with a speed that left the Doctor breathless. It lashed out, its wings sweeping through the air in a cataclysmic arc. A wave of dark energy surged forth, slamming into the Dalek ranks. The ground shook violently, and the air filled with the screeching of metal as the Daleks' casings crumpled inward under the immense force.

"RETREAT! RETREAT!" the Dalek Commander shrieked, attempting to back away, but it was too late. The Death Moth's energy wave struck, engulfing it in a blinding burst of light. The Dalek's shell twisted and collapsed, its eyestalk flickering before shattering into fragments.

The Doctor stood frozen, shielding his eyes from the brilliance of the destruction. In mere moments, the entire Dalek contingent was reduced to a field of mangled metal and debris, their screams echoing in the stillness before fading into silence.

When the light dimmed, the Doctor lowered his arm, his gaze fixed on the Death Moth hovering before him. The creature's eyes glowed softly, its wings beating in slow, rhythmic motions. The Doctor felt a strange sensation—a connection, as if the moth was studying him, weighing his presence and intent.

"You... spared me," the Doctor said quietly, his voice trembling with a mixture of awe and confusion. "Why?"

The Death Moth remained silent, its eyes fixed on him. The Doctor could sense its consciousness pressing into his own, vast and ancient, but not hostile. It was as if the creature recognized something within him, something that resonated with its own purpose.

"BALANCE... IS... INCOMPLETE," it intoned, its voice echoing in the air around them. "YOU... SEEK... RESTORATION."

The Doctor nodded slowly, understanding dawning on him. "Yes," he replied, his voice steady. "I seek restoration, not destruction. Balance isn't just about erasing what disrupts—it's about guiding things back to a natural order."

The Death Moth's form flickered, its light dimming and brightening as it considered his words. Then, it began to ascend, its wings folding around its body. *"YOU... WILL... GUIDE,"* it intoned softly, before vanishing into the sky, leaving behind an eerie stillness.

The Doctor let out a breath he hadn't realized he was holding. "Well," he muttered, rubbing his temples, "that was... something."

Kelnar emerged from the shadows, his eyes wide with shock. "Doctor, it... it spared you. Why?"

The Doctor turned to him, a faint smile playing on his lips. "It seems," he said thoughtfully, "that the Death Moth and I have an understanding. It recognizes that I'm not here to destroy or control, but to restore."

Kelnar glanced nervously at the remains of the Daleks. "And what about them?"

The Doctor sighed, looking at the twisted metal scattered around them. "The Daleks played with forces they didn't understand, and they paid the price. The Death Moth acted to maintain the balance, as it always does. But the fact that it spared me..."

He paused, his gaze drifting to the sky. "It means it's willing to listen. To learn. To change."

Kelnar nodded slowly. "So, what do we do now?"

The Doctor straightened, his eyes filled with determination. "Now, we get to work. We guide this world back to balance, not through destruction, but through understanding and growth. And maybe, just maybe, we show the universe that even forces like the Death Moth can evolve."

As they began to walk away from the battlefield, the Doctor couldn't help but glance back at the horizon. The Death Moth had intervened to save him, and in doing so, it had acknowledged something greater than mere survival. It had acknowledged the possibility of a different kind of balance—a balance forged not through fear and annihilation, but through restoration and harmony.

And the Doctor was determined to see that possibility through, no matter what challenges lay ahead.

Chapter 13: The Moth's Memory

The air in the shadow world grew colder as the Doctor and Kelnar made their way back to the ancient temple. The Doctor walked with purpose, his eyes gleaming with the fire of discovery. His encounter with the Death Moth had left him with an unsettling realization: the creature had spared him not out of mere indifference, but because it had recognized his intentions. It had communicated with him in a way that hinted at a deeper consciousness. He needed to know more.

"We're heading back to the Heart of Shadows," the Doctor said abruptly, glancing at Kelnar. "There's more to the Death Moth than we've realized. It's not just a force of balance; it's something much more complex."

Kelnar frowned, struggling to keep up with the Doctor's quick pace. "What do you mean? You've seen its power—it destroys everything that disrupts the balance."

The Doctor shook his head. "Yes, it destroys, but there's a pattern, a purpose behind it. When it confronted me earlier, I felt it... thinking. It wasn't just reacting; it was weighing, considering. And when it spoke, it didn't just talk about balance—it mentioned restoration."

They reached the temple entrance, its looming shadow casting an aura of foreboding over the ruins. The Doctor didn't hesitate, striding inside with Kelnar close behind. The passageways seemed to twist and echo around them, the walls lined with ancient carvings depicting the cycles of life, death, and rebirth.

"The Heart of Shadows," Kelnar murmured, his eyes scanning the symbols. "It's where the Death Moth draws its power, isn't it?"

"Yes," the Doctor replied, stopping before a massive stone door that led to the heart chamber. "But it's more than just a power source. It's a link to the moth itself. I believe the Death Moth has a consciousness, and that consciousness is stored within this nexus."

Kelnar's eyes widened. "You think it has... memories?"

The Doctor glanced at him, his expression grim. "Yes. Memories of every world, every civilization it has encountered and, regrettably, destroyed. It doesn't just eradicate; it preserves. I need to access those memories if we're to understand its true nature."

Raising his sonic screwdriver, the Doctor activated the door's mechanism. It slid open with a deep rumble, revealing the inner chamber. At its center swirled the Heart of Shadows, a vortex of light and darkness that pulsed with an otherworldly energy. The Doctor approached it cautiously, his eyes locked on the swirling mass.

"Time to have a conversation," he muttered, holding up his screwdriver to scan the energy. A series of high-pitched whirs and clicks emanated from the device as it began to interface with the vortex. The chamber dimmed as the energy within the Heart intensified, reacting to the Doctor's presence.

Kelnar watched, his face pale. "Doctor, what are you doing?"

The Doctor didn't look back. "I'm establishing a connection," he said, his voice strained with concentration. "If the Death Moth has memories, they're in here, stored within the fabric of this world. I need to access them, to understand why it does what it does."

The room vibrated, and the air grew thick with tension. The vortex's swirling patterns became erratic, and the light it emitted grew brighter, casting eerie shadows across the chamber walls. Then, suddenly, everything went silent.

The Doctor gasped, his eyes widening as his mind was flooded with images. It was as if a door had been opened within his consciousness, revealing an endless archive of memories—countless civilizations, worlds, and beings, all imprinted within the energy of the Death Moth.

"What...?" he breathed, his voice barely a whisper. "What is this?"

He was no longer in the temple. His mind had been pulled into a vast expanse of stars and darkness. Around him, he saw visions of worlds, some vibrant with life, others crumbling into dust. The images moved like waves, each one carrying fragments of memories: cities towering under alien suns, cultures thriving in harmony with their environments, and then... collapse. Catastrophes, wars, invasions—moments of imbalance that drew the Death Moth like a beacon.

The Doctor turned slowly, his gaze sweeping over the expanse. "You... remember," he said aloud, sensing the presence of the Death Moth around him. "You remember everything."

A soft hum filled the air, and the darkness before him coalesced into the familiar shape of the Death Moth. Its wings glowed faintly, casting an ethereal light. The Doctor felt its consciousness pressing into his own, vast and ancient, like an ocean of thought.

"BALANCE... IS... PRESERVATION," the Death Moth intoned, its voice echoing through the void. "MEMORIES... OF THOSE WHO... HAVE FALLEN... MUST BE KEPT."

The Doctor blinked, piecing together the fragments of what he was seeing and hearing. "You're not just a force of destruction," he murmured. "You're a... historian. You carry the memories of the civilizations you've encountered. When you 'restore balance,' you're not wiping them out completely. You're... preserving them in a way."

The Death Moth's form flickered, its eyes glowing softly. "MEMORIES... ARE... THE ESSENCE OF... EXISTENCE. TO DESTROY... WITHOUT REMEMBRANCE... IS TO ERASE... THE PURPOSE OF... BALANCE."

The Doctor felt a chill run down his spine. "Then that's why you acted so swiftly with the Daleks and Cybermen," he realized. "They threatened to disrupt the natural order, to dominate and erase. You intervened not just to restore balance but to ensure that their memory would not be one of unchecked conquest."

"CORRECT," the Death Moth replied, its voice resonating through the Doctor's mind. "BALANCE REQUIRES... REMEMBRANCE. TO PRESERVE THE... ESSENCE... OF LIFE... IN ALL ITS FORMS."

The Doctor's hearts pounded in his chest as he absorbed the implications. The Death Moth wasn't a mere cosmic reaper; it was a guardian of history. It acted not only to correct imbalances but also to ensure that the legacy of every world, every species, was remembered in the cosmic tapestry.

"But you... destroy so much," the Doctor said, his voice trembling. "If preservation is your purpose, then why must it come with such devastation?"

The Death Moth's eyes flared, and the darkness around them rippled. "DESTRUCTION IS... NOT THE END," it intoned. "IT IS... TRANSITION. THE MEMORIES... OF WHAT ONCE WAS... GIVE BIRTH TO... WHAT WILL BE."

The Doctor took a step back, his mind racing. "So, in your destruction, you're also planting the seeds for the future," he whispered. "A way for new life to grow from the remnants of the old. You carry the memories of those who have fallen so that something new can learn from them, evolve from them."

The Death Moth's wings spread wide, their light intensifying. "EXISTENCE IS... A CYCLE. BALANCE IS... THE REMEMBRANCE OF... THE PAST... TO GUIDE... THE FUTURE."

The Doctor closed his eyes, a wave of understanding washing over him. "You're not a harbinger of doom," he murmured. "You're a guardian of the universe's story. And you're trying to ensure that every story, no matter how tragic, has a chance to be remembered and to influence what comes next."

A silence settled between them, the weight of the revelations pressing down on the Doctor's shoulders. He opened his eyes, meeting the Death Moth's gaze. "You act as you must, but you don't act without thought," he said softly. "You preserve history even as you enforce balance. But... you can choose how you intervene."

The Death Moth's form dimmed slightly, its wings folding around its body. "BALANCE IS... A CHOICE," it intoned, the light in its eyes flickering. "HOW IT IS... RESTORED... DEPENDS ON... THE NATURE... OF THOSE WHO... SEEK TO... DISRUPT IT."

The Doctor nodded, his expression resolute. "Then let's choose a different path this time," he said firmly. "Let's use your memories not as a record of devastation, but as a guide for renewal. Let's help this world learn from its past, so it doesn't need to be wiped clean."

The Death Moth remained silent, its wings beating slowly. The Doctor sensed a shift in its presence, a subtle change in its perception. For a moment, he felt the immense burden it carried—the countless memories of civilizations, the weight of maintaining a cosmic balance that was never static.

"GUIDANCE..." it murmured, its voice like a whisper across the void. "THE FUTURE... CAN LEARN FROM... THE PAST."

The Doctor exhaled slowly, feeling a glimmer of hope. "Yes," he agreed. "We can guide this world back to balance without destroying it. And you... you can help us do that, not as a destroyer, but as a keeper of history."

The Death Moth's form began to fade, its light receding into the darkness. "REMEMBRANCE... WILL GUIDE... BALANCE," it intoned softly. "THE PAST WILL... SHAPE THE... FUTURE."

The visions around the Doctor blurred, the stars and memories dissolving into a swirl of light and shadow. He felt himself being pulled back, the connection to the Heart of Shadows slowly closing. Then, with a rush of sensation, he was back in the temple chamber, gasping for breath as the vortex dimmed.

"Doctor!" Kelnar cried, rushing forward. "Are you alright?"

The Doctor nodded weakly, leaning on the temple wall for support. "Yes," he panted, his eyes wide with the enormity of what he had just experienced. "I'm... alright. But we have much to do. The Death Moth isn't just a destroyer; it's a keeper of memories. It carries the history of the civilizations it encounters, preserving them even as it enforces balance."

Kelnar stared at him, bewildered. "Then... what does that mean for us?"

"It means," the Doctor replied, straightening up, "that we have a chance to restore this world, to learn from its past and avoid its mistakes. The Death Moth is willing to guide us, to show us the way. But we have to be ready to listen, to remember."

He turned to the vortex, his eyes gleaming with determination. "Balance isn't just about correction. It's about learning, preserving the lessons of history so that we can build a future that doesn't repeat the same mistakes."

Kelnar nodded slowly, hope flickering in his eyes. "Then let's do it, Doctor. Let's build that future."

The Doctor smiled, the weight of the Death Moth's memories still pressing on his mind, but now tempered with the resolve to guide them toward renewal. "Yes," he said quietly. "Let's remember, and let's rebuild."

And so, the Doctor and Kelnar left the chamber, carrying with them not just the hope of a restored balance but the knowledge that the Death Moth was more than a harbinger of destruction. It was a keeper of history, a force that preserved the past so that the future could learn and grow. And now, the Doctor was determined to ensure that the next chapter in that story would be one of rebirth, not ruin.

Chapter 14: A Time Lord's Bargain

The light of the setting stars in the shadow world dimmed as the Doctor emerged from the ancient temple, his expression a mixture of resolve and contemplation. The weight of the Death Moth's memories still pressed upon him, filling his mind with echoes of countless civilizations that had been consumed and preserved within its cosmic consciousness. The revelation of the moth as not merely a destroyer but as a keeper of history had changed everything. The creature's actions were not driven by malice; they were an expression of an ancient, almost solemn duty to maintain balance.

Kelnar stood nearby, his eyes fixed on the Doctor. "What now, Doctor? If the Death Moth is a keeper of memories, how do we use that knowledge to stop it from destroying everything?"

The Doctor paused, staring out across the ruins of the shadow world. He felt the vastness of the Death Moth's purpose, a purpose that intersected with his own in ways he hadn't fully grasped before. "We don't stop it," he said slowly, his eyes darkening with thought. "We guide it."

Kelnar frowned. "Guide it? How do we do that?"

The Doctor turned to him, his expression set with determination. "I need to communicate with it directly, to use my Time Lord abilities to reach into its consciousness and make it see another path. The moth is bound to its purpose, but that purpose can evolve. And I'm going to offer it a bargain."

Kelnar's eyes widened. "A bargain? With that creature? You're mad."

The Doctor chuckled dryly. "Yes, well, it wouldn't be the first time, would it?" His expression turned serious again as he gazed up at the sky, where the moth had vanished. "I need to show it that there's a way to fulfill its mission without endless destruction. If I can make it see that balance is not just a reset but a process of renewal, it might listen."

"And what's the bargain?" Kelnar asked, apprehensive.

The Doctor's eyes gleamed. "Simple: I help it restore balance to this world and others, but without unnecessary eradication. In return, it co-operates with me to find ways of correcting imbalances without destroying the civilizations it encounters."

Kelnar looked at him skeptically. "You really think it will listen to you?"

"It has to," the Doctor replied, his voice filled with a mix of hope and urgency. "Because if it doesn't, then everything it has preserved, every memory it holds, will be for nothing. It preserves history, yes, but history that endlessly repeats its own failures is no better than oblivion. I need to make it understand that."

With that, the Doctor took a deep breath and raised his hands to the sky, his gaze focused and intense. "Alright, you cosmic force of balance," he murmured, closing his eyes. "It's time we had a proper conversation."

The air around him began to hum, vibrating with a strange energy. Kelnar stepped back, his eyes wide as a gust of wind swept through the ruins, swirling dust and debris around the Doctor. The ground trembled slightly, and the temperature dropped, signaling the approach of the Death Moth.

From the shadows above, a faint glow appeared, growing brighter with each passing second. The Doctor felt the presence of the creature before he saw it—a vast consciousness pressing against his mind, ancient and relentless. He reached out with his own Time Lord senses, extending his thoughts toward the entity.

The Death Moth materialized, descending from the sky with an almost solemn grace. Its wings spread wide, casting a pale, ethereal light across the ruins. It hovered before the Doctor, its eyes glowing softly as it regarded him with an unfathomable gaze.

"You've come," the Doctor said softly, opening his eyes to meet the creature's gaze. "I need to speak with you, not as a force of destruction, but as a keeper of history. We have more in common than you might think."

The Death Moth's form rippled, the air around it growing colder. *"TIME LORD... YOU SEEK... UNDERSTANDING,"* it intoned, its voice echoing through the air like a whisper from the depths of the universe. *"BALANCE... IS... A CYCLE."*

The Doctor nodded, stepping closer. "Yes, it is. But that cycle doesn't have to end in complete annihilation. I've seen your memories. You've preserved the essence of countless civilizations, even as you've corrected the imbalances they created. I'm here to offer you a different way."

The moth's eyes flickered, its wings beating slowly. *"BALANCE... REQUIRES... CORRECTION,"* it replied. *"CORRECTION... IS... DESTRUCTION."*

"Not necessarily," the Doctor countered, his voice rising with conviction. "Destruction can be a part of correction, yes, but it's not the only path. What if, instead of obliterating entire civilizations, you guided them toward restoring balance themselves? Help them understand their mistakes, show them how to change. Isn't that the true essence of preservation?"

The Death Moth remained silent, its eyes fixed on the Doctor. He felt its consciousness probing his mind, sifting through his thoughts and memories. He allowed it to see his own experiences, his triumphs and failures, his endless struggle to maintain a balance between chaos and order.

"You see it, don't you?" the Doctor pressed, his tone softer now. "I've spent lifetimes correcting the universe's imbalances, but I've learned that force alone isn't enough. It's about guiding, teaching, helping civilizations to grow beyond their mistakes. You've preserved the memory of every world you've encountered, but what if you could preserve their future as well?"

The air around them crackled with energy, and the Death Moth's form shimmered. *"GUIDANCE... REQUIRES... CHANGE,"* it intoned. *"CHANGE IS... UNCERTAIN."*

"Yes," the Doctor agreed, his voice firm. "Change is uncertain. It's terrifying, messy, and sometimes painful. But it's also the only way forward. I'm not asking you to abandon your purpose—I'm asking you to adapt it. To work with me. Together, we can restore balance to this world and others without unnecessary destruction."

The moth's wings beat more rapidly, sending gusts of wind swirling around them. The Doctor could sense its conflict, the ancient patterns of its purpose clashing with the new possibility he was presenting.

"Think of it as an evolution," the Doctor continued, his eyes blazing with intensity. "Your existence is built on cycles, on the preservation of history. But history isn't static; it changes, evolves. This is your chance to be part of that evolution. I'm offering you a way to fulfill your purpose while allowing the worlds you encounter to learn, to grow."

The Death Moth hovered silently, its light dimming and brightening as it processed his words. The Doctor felt its consciousness pressing into his own, a sensation both cold and strangely comforting, as if it were seeking to understand the depths of his intentions.

"A... BARGAIN," the moth intoned at last, its voice like the rustling of ancient leaves. "GUIDE THE... RESTORATION... AND WE WILL... ASSIST. BUT IF... BALANCE CANNOT... BE ACHIEVED..."

The Doctor nodded, understanding the unspoken condition. "If balance cannot be achieved," he said quietly, "then we will face the consequences together. But I believe we can do it. I believe that with your guidance, we can teach the universe a new way to maintain balance."

The Death Moth's eyes glowed brighter, its wings folding around its body as it descended closer to the Doctor. He felt its presence wrapping around his mind, a vast ocean of memories and thoughts intermingling with his own. For a brief moment, he glimpsed its essence—an ancient consciousness burdened by the duty to correct the universe's course.

"TIME LORD... WE ACCEPT... YOUR BARGAIN," it intoned, its voice reverberating through the air. "BALANCE WILL... BE RE-

STORED... THROUGH... GUIDANCE. BUT KNOW THIS... FAIL-URE WILL... BRING... CONSEQUENCES."

The Doctor exhaled slowly, relief washing over him. "Understood," he replied, his voice steady. "Then let's begin."

The Death Moth's form shimmered, and it began to ascend, its wings unfurling like a vast, cosmic curtain. The air around them grew warmer, the oppressive chill lifting as the moth retreated into the sky. It left behind a faint glow, a lingering presence that signaled its willingness to work alongside the Doctor.

Kelnar approached cautiously, his eyes wide with awe. "Doctor, did it... agree?"

The Doctor nodded, his expression weary but resolute. "Yes," he confirmed. "It's agreed to help restore balance without unnecessary destruction. But it won't be easy. We have to show the universe that it can learn, that it can grow without resorting to annihilation."

Kelnar looked at him, a flicker of hope in his eyes. "And you think we can do it?"

The Doctor managed a small smile. "We have to. Because if we fail, the Death Moth will enforce balance in the only way it knows—through devastation. This is our chance to change that, to guide the universe toward a new kind of harmony."

He turned to the horizon, where the Death Moth had vanished. "It's a Time Lord's bargain," he said quietly. "A promise that we'll guide this world—and others—toward balance. And in return, the moth will learn to be more than just a force of destruction. It will become a guardian of renewal."

As they stood there, the shadows around them began to recede, the faint glow of the Death Moth lingering in the sky. It was a new beginning, a fragile hope that balance could be achieved without erasing everything in its path. The Doctor was determined to see this through, to uphold his side of the bargain and show that even the cosmos itself could learn to change.

And with that resolve, he turned and began to lead the way forward, ready to guide the shadow world—and the Death Moth—toward a future that embraced restoration over ruin.

Chapter 15: The Daleks' Final Assault

The shadow world had fallen into an uneasy quiet, a calm that preceded the storm everyone felt brewing. The Doctor stood at the edge of the ruins, gazing into the distance with an unsettling tension gnawing at his thoughts. Despite the fragile accord he had established with the Death Moth, he knew the Daleks were far from finished. Desperation was a powerful motivator, and the Daleks, fueled by their arrogance and singular drive for domination, were preparing for a final gambit.

Kelnar approached, his face etched with concern. "Doctor, I've been scouting the outskirts," he began, his voice low. "The Daleks... they're massing. There are hundreds of them, and they're bringing something big. I've never seen weapons like these before."

The Doctor turned to him, his eyes narrowing. "I was afraid of this," he muttered. "The Daleks never give up, especially when they're so close to what they perceive as ultimate power. They'll try to take the Death Moth by force, regardless of the consequences."

"What do we do?" Kelnar asked, his voice tinged with fear. "If they attack the Death Moth, won't it just retaliate like before?"

The Doctor nodded grimly. "Yes, but this time, the Daleks are bringing a much larger force. They're desperate, which means they're dangerous. They've likely developed some kind of experimental weaponry to try and trap or neutralize the moth." He paused, his mind racing through possibilities. "But the problem with desperation, Kelnar, is that it often leads to reckless decisions."

He took a deep breath and straightened, his eyes hardening with resolve. "We have to be ready. The Daleks' final assault could trigger the moth into a full-scale reaction, something that could potentially tear this world apart."

As he spoke, a low, rhythmic droning filled the air, growing louder and more ominous. The ground beneath their feet began to vibrate as a fleet of Dalek ships emerged from the horizon, their metallic hulls glinting in the dim light of the shadow world. Swarming around the ships were hundreds of Daleks, gliding forward with their weapons primed and ready.

The Doctor squinted, raising his sonic screwdriver to scan the approaching armada. His eyes widened at the results. "Oh, they've really gone all out this time," he muttered. "Those ships are carrying containment fields powered by temporal energy. They're going to try to trap the Death Moth within a time-locked stasis."

Kelnar paled. "Can they do that?"

The Doctor shook his head, his expression grave. "Theoretically, yes. Temporarily. But using that kind of technology on a force like the Death Moth is like trying to hold a hurricane in a glass jar. If they succeed in trapping it, the containment field will become unstable. It will backfire, and when it does, it will release a cataclysmic wave of energy."

The Daleks closed in, their fleet spreading out to encircle the area. A piercing, metallic voice filled the air, echoing across the ruins. "DOCTOR! YOU WILL SURRENDER THE DEATH MOTH TO THE DALEK EMPIRE!"

The Doctor stepped forward, his hearts pounding as he faced the encroaching Dalek forces. "This is madness!" he shouted. "You can't control the Death Moth! If you trap it, you'll destabilize the entire world, maybe even rip a hole in reality itself!"

"YOUR DEFIANCE IS FUTILE!" the lead Dalek barked, its eyestalk swiveling toward him. "THE DEATH MOTH IS... POWER! THE DALEKS WILL... HARNESS THAT POWER OR... EXTERMINATE IT!"

The Doctor clenched his fists, his mind racing through potential responses. "Don't you understand?" he yelled. "The Death Moth isn't just energy; it's a conscious force of balance! If you trap it, you disrupt that balance and doom yourselves in the process!"

"THE DALEK EMPIRE IS... SUPREME!" the Dalek Commander screeched. "PREPARE TO... INITIATE CONTAINMENT PROTOCOL!"

The ships overhead began to emit a low hum, and arcs of blue energy surged across their surfaces. The Doctor could see the faint outlines of a containment field forming, powered by temporal stabilizers designed to lock the Death Moth in stasis. His eyes widened in horror as the realization of their plan sank in.

"They're actually going to do it," he muttered, gripping his sonic screwdriver. "They're going to try to time-lock the moth."

He turned to Kelnar, his expression fierce. "Get to cover!" he commanded. "If this goes wrong—and it will—we need to be ready for the fallout."

Kelnar nodded and ran toward the remnants of a stone structure, ducking behind it as the air around them began to crackle with static energy. The Doctor stood his ground, his gaze fixed on the sky where the Dalek ships were converging.

"Here we go," he murmured, his grip tightening on the screwdriver.

A beam of energy shot down from the lead Dalek ship, striking the ground in a blinding flash. A deep hum resonated through the air, and from the epicenter of the beam, a shimmering dome of light began to expand, spreading out toward the sky. The containment field was forming, growing larger with every passing second.

The Doctor felt the temperature drop, and the ground beneath him shook violently. He glanced upward and saw it—the Death Moth, descending from the dark clouds above. Its wings spread wide, glowing with a brilliant, ethereal light that cut through the encroaching containment field like a knife.

"INITIATE FULL CONTAINMENT!" the Dalek Commander screeched. "TRAP THE ENTITY!"

The ships intensified their energy output, pouring more power into the containment field. The dome of light surged upward, attempting to encase the Death Moth within its temporal lock. For a brief moment, it seemed as though they might succeed. The moth's form flickered, its wings slowing as the temporal energy pressed against it.

But then, something changed. The Death Moth's eyes blazed with an intense light, and the air around it rippled with a wave of dark energy. The containment field began to waver, cracks appearing in its surface as it struggled to hold the moth in place.

"WARNING! CONTAINMENT FIELD... UNSTABLE!" a Dalek screeched, panic evident in its voice.

"STABILIZE THE FIELD!" the Dalek Commander ordered, its eyestalk swiveling frantically. "DO NOT... LET IT ESCAPE!"

The Doctor shook his head, feeling the building energy in the air. "You've lost control," he muttered. "Now you're going to see the consequences of your arrogance."

The Death Moth spread its wings wide, and a deafening roar filled the air. A surge of raw, unbridled power erupted from its body, crashing into the containment field like a tidal wave. The dome shattered, fragments of temporal energy scattering across the sky in blinding flashes.

"NOOO!" the Dalek Commander screamed. "CONTAINMENT... FAILURE!"

The release of energy triggered a chain reaction. The temporal stabilizers aboard the Dalek ships began to overload, arcs of blue lightning dancing across their hulls. The ships shook violently, and one by one, they exploded in bursts of white-hot light, sending debris raining down upon the ruins below.

The ground quaked as shockwaves from the explosions rippled outward, knocking Daleks to the ground. They screeched in terror, their cries of "EXTERMINATE!" turning into distorted howls as they were caught in the blast radius.

The Death Moth descended, its wings beating furiously as it unleashed another wave of energy. This time, the force was directed at the Dalek ground forces. Metal casings crumpled inward, and the air was filled with the cacophony of screeching metal and desperate, dying cries.

"RETREAT! RETREAT!" the Dalek Commander bellowed, trying to flee. But it was too late. The Death Moth's energy engulfed it, crushing its form into a twisted mass of metal.

The Doctor stood amidst the chaos, his eyes fixed on the unfolding carnage. He had warned them, tried to stop them, but the Daleks had been blinded by their desire for power. Now, they were paying the ultimate price for their hubris.

Finally, the light dimmed, and the ground fell silent. The Dalek ships had been reduced to smoldering wrecks, and the remaining Daleks lay scattered, their casings shattered and lifeless. The Death Moth hovered above the battlefield, its wings slowing as it surveyed the destruction.

The Doctor took a deep breath, stepping forward. "It's done," he said softly, his voice tinged with sorrow. "The balance has been restored, but at what cost?"

The Death Moth turned its gaze toward him, its eyes glowing softly. *"THEY SOUGHT... TO DOMINATE,"* it intoned, its voice echoing through the ruins. *"BALANCE REQUIRED... CORRECTION."*

The Doctor nodded, feeling the weight of the truth in its words. "Yes," he replied quietly. "They did. But I wish it hadn't come to this."

The moth's wings beat slowly, casting long shadows across the battlefield. *"CORRECTION IS... A CHOICE,"* it murmured. *"DESTRUCTION WAS... THEIR PATH."*

The Doctor looked up at it, his eyes reflecting the light of its wings. "And what about our path?" he asked. "The bargain we made? Can we still find a way to guide this world back to balance without more destruction?"

The Death Moth hovered silently, its form shimmering. Then, it began to ascend, its light growing fainter as it rose into the sky. *"BALANCE IS... RESTORED... FOR NOW,"* it intoned. *"GUIDANCE WILL... CONTINUE."*

As the moth vanished into the clouds, the Doctor let out a slow breath, turning to face the ruins around him. The Daleks' final assault had been their undoing, but it had also reaffirmed the fragile nature of the balance they sought to maintain.

Kelnar approached cautiously, his eyes wide with awe. "Doctor, is it... over?"

The Doctor nodded, his expression grim. "For now, yes. The Daleks' arrogance led them to their downfall. The Death Moth has corrected the imbalance they caused, but it won't stay quiet forever. It's up to us to ensure that the world finds a way to maintain balance without inviting its wrath again."

Kelnar looked out over the battlefield, his face pale. "And if it doesn't?"

"Then," the Doctor said quietly, "the Death Moth will return. And next time, it may not be so merciful."

With those words hanging in the air, the Doctor turned away from the ruins, his mind already racing with plans to guide this world—and others—toward a future where balance was not enforced through annihilation, but through understanding and growth.

It was a daunting task, but it was one he was willing to undertake. Because now, more than ever, he understood the stakes: the Death Moth was not just a force to be feared; it was a force to be guided, a cosmic entity that could evolve—if only the universe could learn to evolve with it.

Chapter 16: The Wrath of the Moth

The air in the shadow world grew tense, an electric charge building as if the entire planet was holding its breath. The Doctor stood on a crumbling precipice, his eyes scanning the sky where dark clouds swirled ominously. The Dalek fleet had been decimated in their failed final assault, but a few stragglers remained, desperately regrouping in a last-ditch effort to escape the devastation they had wrought.

"Doctor," Kelnar called out as he stumbled up beside him, his face streaked with dirt and fear. "What's happening? The sky... it's changing."

The Doctor's gaze remained fixed on the horizon. "The Death Moth," he muttered, almost to himself. "It's preparing to unleash its full power. The Daleks pushed it too far, and now they're about to witness the true consequence of their actions."

Kelnar paled. "But... we managed to talk to it before. Can't you stop it now?"

The Doctor shook his head, his expression grim. "Not this time. The moth's purpose is balance, and the Daleks have thrown the scales too far out of line. It gave them a chance to retreat, but they refused. Now, it's going to finish what they started."

In the distance, the Dalek ships huddled together, their hulls battered and scarred from the earlier battle. They emitted a series of frantic communications, their metallic voices crackling through the static-filled air.

"DALEK FORCES... REGROUPING!" one of them screamed. "RETREAT TO SECTOR 9! INITIATE... EMERGENCY HYPER-DRIVE!"

The Doctor frowned, raising his sonic screwdriver to scan the energy patterns in the sky. "They're trying to escape," he murmured, his voice tinged with both frustration and pity. "But they're too late. They've already triggered the moth's wrath."

A deep hum resonated from the sky, growing louder with each passing second. The clouds above the Dalek fleet began to swirl, forming a massive vortex that crackled with streaks of lightning. From within this maelstrom, a glow emerged—faint at first but intensifying rapidly, casting a cold, spectral light across the landscape.

The Death Moth descended, its wings spreading wide, glowing with an eerie, ethereal brilliance. Its eyes blazed like stars, casting twin beams of light that swept across the Dalek fleet, freezing them in place.

The Daleks reacted instantly, their eyestalks swiveling frantically. "ALERT! ALERT!" the lead Dalek screamed. "UNKNOWN ENTITY... APPROACHING! INITIATE... DEFENSIVE MANEUVERS!"

The ships pivoted, their energy weapons charging to maximum capacity. Arcs of blue electricity crackled along their surfaces as they prepared to fire. But the Death Moth moved faster than their targeting systems could react. It swooped down in a blur of motion, its wings beating with the force of a hurricane.

The air itself seemed to tear open as a shockwave of dark energy burst from the moth's form, slamming into the Dalek ships. The ground shook violently, and a deafening roar filled the air, drowning out the panicked cries of the Daleks.

"SHIELDS FAILING!" a Dalek shrieked. "UNABLE TO... CONTAIN... THE ENTITY!"

The Doctor watched, his hearts pounding in his chest. He had seen the moth's power before, but never like this. It was unleashing its full might, a force of nature in its most primal and devastating form. There was a terrible beauty to it, an awe-inspiring yet horrifying display of cosmic balance in action.

"Doctor!" Kelnar shouted over the cacophony. "What's it doing?"

"It's correcting the imbalance," the Doctor replied, his voice strained. "The Daleks have defied every natural law in their lust for power, and the moth is delivering the final judgment."

With a sound like the shattering of glass, the containment fields around the Dalek ships broke apart, fragments of blue energy scattering into the sky. The moth's eyes flared brighter, and it unleashed another wave of dark energy that surged outward, enveloping the fleet.

The Dalek ships buckled under the onslaught, their hulls warping and crumpling as if crushed by an invisible fist. Explosions rippled through their ranks, and one by one, they disintegrated in blinding flashes of light. The air was filled with the screeching of metal and the last, desperate cries of the Daleks.

"NOOO!" the lead Dalek screamed. "THIS IS... IMPOSSIBLE! WE ARE... THE DALEK EMPIRE! WE... ARE... SUP—"

Its voice was abruptly cut off as the moth's energy wave engulfed it, collapsing its form into a mass of molten metal. The remnants of the Dalek fleet shattered, pieces of their once-mighty war machines raining down upon the ruins in a storm of debris.

The Doctor stood motionless, his eyes locked on the devastation unfolding before him. The moth hovered above the battlefield, its wings beating slowly, rhythmically. The ground beneath it was scorched, the air charged with residual energy that crackled and hummed with an unsettling intensity.

"They're gone," Kelnar breathed, his voice barely audible in the aftermath of the storm. "The Daleks... they're really gone."

The Doctor nodded, his expression somber. "Yes," he said quietly. "The Death Moth has seen to that. It's finished what they started."

He took a step forward, raising his gaze to the creature that now floated silently above the ruins. "You've completed your task," he called out, his voice steady but edged with an undercurrent of emotion. "You've restored the balance."

The Death Moth turned its glowing eyes toward him, the air around them growing cold. *"BALANCE IS... RESTORED,"* it intoned, its voice echoing through the ruins like a ghostly whisper. *"THE THREAT... IS... NO MORE."*

The Doctor swallowed, feeling a knot of conflicting emotions in his chest. "You didn't just destroy them," he said, his voice trembling slightly. "You erased them. Not just as a threat, but as a force that could tip the universe into chaos. It was necessary, but... it was also tragic."

The moth's form flickered, its wings folding slightly as it seemed to contemplate his words. *"DESTRUCTION IS... A PART OF... BALANCE,"* it replied. *"SOME MUST FALL... FOR OTHERS TO... RISE."*

The Doctor nodded slowly. "Yes, but it doesn't make it any easier to watch," he admitted. "There's always a cost, isn't there? Even when it's necessary, even when it's right."

"THE COST IS... THE BURDEN OF... EXISTENCE," the moth murmured, its voice carrying the weight of countless ages. *"BUT REMEMBER... THE MEMORY OF... WHAT ONCE WAS... GUIDES THE... FUTURE."*

The Doctor sighed, feeling the gravity of those words settle over him. "You're right," he said softly. "You've preserved their memory, even as you've erased their threat. And that's what we must hold onto: the lessons of what has been lost, so that we don't repeat the same mistakes."

The Death Moth's eyes dimmed, its wings beating gently as it began to ascend into the sky. *"THE UNIVERSE WILL... CONTINUE,"* it intoned. *"BALANCE WILL... EVOLVE. AND YOU... TIME LORD... SHALL GUIDE."*

The Doctor watched as the moth disappeared into the swirling clouds above, its presence leaving behind a lingering, ghostly light. For a moment, the world was utterly still, the echoes of the moth's power reverberating through the air.

Kelnar approached cautiously, his face a mixture of awe and fear. "Is it... over?" he asked, his voice unsteady.

The Doctor turned to him, his expression solemn but resolute. "For now, yes," he replied. "The Death Moth has eradicated the last of the Daleks. It's restored the balance, but it's also reminded us of the cost that comes with defying the natural order."

Kelnar looked at the smoldering remains scattered across the ruins. "But was it worth it?"

The Doctor sighed, his gaze drifting to the horizon. "That's a question we'll be asking for a long time," he admitted. "The Daleks were a threat that couldn't be allowed to persist. Their destruction was necessary to prevent even greater chaos. But worth it? That's harder to say. All we can do now is learn from this, carry the memory forward, and ensure that the future doesn't repeat these same mistakes."

Kelnar nodded slowly, his eyes filled with a mixture of sorrow and understanding. "And what about the moth? Will it return?"

The Doctor turned away from the battlefield, his coat billowing slightly in the wind. "It will," he said, his voice firm. "Because balance is never permanent. It's a constant struggle, a dance between order and chaos. But we've made a bargain, the moth and I. I will guide, and it will watch. Together, we'll seek to restore harmony without resorting to annihilation."

He started walking, gesturing for Kelnar to follow. "Come on," he said, his tone lighter but still carrying the weight of recent events. "We have a lot of work to do. The world won't rebuild itself, and we need to show that balance can be achieved without summoning the moth's wrath again."

As they moved away from the ruins, the Doctor couldn't help but glance back one last time. The Death Moth's wrath had been absolute, a force of cosmic judgment that had wiped away the Daleks' final assault. But within that terrible display of power lay a deeper truth—a reminder that balance, while often harsh, was essential to the survival of the universe.

And now, it was his task to guide that balance toward a future where such destruction was no longer necessary.

Chapter 17: The Rebirth of Worlds

The landscape of the shadow world was silent, the aftermath of the Death Moth's wrath leaving an eerie stillness in the air. The Doctor stood at the edge of a vast, scorched plain, his eyes scanning the horizon. Here, he had witnessed the Death Moth's full might as it decimated the Dalek fleet, ensuring that balance was restored. Yet, the sense of finality brought little comfort. Destruction alone wasn't enough; now, they had to turn the tides toward renewal.

Kelnar walked up beside him, looking out over the lifeless terrain. "The Daleks and Cybermen are gone," he said quietly. "But so is everything else. How do we even begin to bring life back to these worlds?"

The Doctor was silent for a moment, contemplating the task before them. Then, he took a deep breath, his gaze hardening with resolve. "We begin by understanding that balance isn't just about destruction; it's about regeneration. The universe thrives on cycles—death gives way to new life, endings become beginnings. And now, it's time to fulfill the other part of our bargain with the Death Moth."

Kelnar looked at him with a mixture of hope and skepticism. "You think it's possible? That the Death Moth can actually... bring life back?"

The Doctor turned to face him, a faint smile tugging at the corners of his mouth. "I think it's more than possible. I think it's essential. The Death Moth isn't just a force of annihilation; it's a keeper of memories, a guardian of the universe's cycles. Now, we need to tap into that energy not to destroy, but to renew."

He raised his hands to the sky, his eyes searching for any sign of the moth's presence. "Death Moth!" he called out, his voice echoing across the barren land. "We've restored balance through destruction, but now we must restore it through creation. We have another part of our bargain to fulfill."

The air around them grew colder, and a faint hum resonated through the earth. From the darkened sky, the familiar glow began to appear, swirling with an ethereal light that descended slowly toward the Doctor and Kelnar. The Death Moth materialized, its wings casting a pale luminescence over the ruined land. It hovered before them, its eyes gleaming like distant stars.

"You came," the Doctor said, lowering his hands. "Good. We've wiped away the remnants of those who threatened the balance. Now it's time to plant the seeds of renewal."

The Death Moth's wings beat gently, stirring a breeze that carried a whisper of life through the scorched air. *"BALANCE IS... NOT JUST... DESTRUCTION,"* it intoned, its voice resonating like a distant echo. *"LIFE MUST... RETURN... TO THE WORLDS THAT WERE... LOST."*

"Yes," the Doctor agreed, taking a step forward. "You've preserved the memories of those worlds within you, haven't you? Every planet you've consumed, every civilization you've encountered—it's all part of your essence. Now, we can use that knowledge to help them bloom again."

Kelnar looked up at the moth, awe written across his face. "You mean... it can revive these worlds?"

The Doctor nodded. "In a way, yes. The Death Moth has absorbed the life force of countless worlds over millennia. It holds within it the essence of what once was. If it releases that energy in the right way, new life can sprout from the remnants of the old."

The Death Moth's eyes flickered, its wings spreading wider as it seemed to contemplate the Doctor's words. *"RENEWAL... IS A RISK,"* it murmured. *"NEW LIFE MAY... FALL INTO... OLD PATTERNS."*

The Doctor raised his head, meeting the creature's gaze. "True," he conceded. "But that's part of existence, isn't it? The risk that we might repeat our mistakes. The challenge is to grow beyond them. To evolve. And that's where you come in, Death Moth. You're not just a harbinger of death; you're a guardian of memory. Guide the new life that rises from these ashes, show them the history they carry, and help them build something better."

A silence settled over the landscape, the air thick with the weight of the moment. The Death Moth hovered above, its form shimmering with an inner light that began to intensify. The Doctor could feel the tension within the creature—the pull between its ancient purpose of correction and this new path of renewal.

"VERY WELL," the moth intoned finally, its voice as soft as the rustling of leaves. *"THE WORLDS WILL BE... REVITALIZED. BUT THEY MUST... LEARN FROM WHAT WAS... LOST."*

The Doctor exhaled, a rush of relief washing over him. "Thank you," he said quietly. "We'll help them, I promise. Together, we'll ensure that what grows here doesn't fall into the same traps as before."

The Death Moth's wings began to beat faster, and a surge of energy rippled through the air. The ground beneath their feet trembled as the moth rose higher, its light growing blindingly bright. Streams of energy poured from its body, cascading down like rivers of molten starlight that spread across the devastated landscape.

"Doctor!" Kelnar cried, stumbling back. "What's happening?"

"Watch," the Doctor replied, his eyes fixed on the unfolding spectacle. "It's releasing the energy it's absorbed over countless ages, the essence of the worlds it's preserved within its being."

The streams of light flowed across the ground, seeping into the cracked earth. Where the energy touched, the soil began to shift, heaving as if awakening from a deep slumber. The Doctor watched in awe as small green shoots emerged from the soil, unfurling into leaves and flowers that swayed in the light of the moth's glow.

Slowly, the barren wasteland began to transform. Grass spread like a verdant carpet over the once-scorched plains, while saplings pushed upward, their branches stretching toward the sky. Rivers of clear, sparkling water carved paths through the landscape, reflecting the moth's brilliance. It was a scene of rebirth, of new life taking root in the ashes of the old.

The Doctor turned, gazing out across the rejuvenating world. "It's happening," he breathed, his voice filled with wonder. "The Death Moth is giving back the life it took. Not exactly the same as before, but something new, something that carries the memory of what once was."

Kelnar looked around, his eyes wide with amazement. "It's... beautiful," he whispered. "I never thought I'd see something like this here."

The Death Moth continued to hover above, its energy pouring out in waves that surged across the horizon. The landscape changed rapidly, forests springing up where there had been only dust, flowers blooming in vibrant colors, and streams gushing with the promise of new ecosystems.

But the Doctor knew that this was more than just a spectacle of nature reclaiming the land. It was a testament to the power of renewal, to the idea that balance was not about restoring what was lost exactly as it was, but about creating something new that could learn from the past.

"Look," he said, pointing toward a cluster of trees that had formed nearby. "The plants are different. They're not the same species that once grew here. They're hybrids, new forms that have adapted to this changed environment."

Kelnar nodded, his face lighting up with realization. "The moth isn't just recreating what was; it's evolving the landscape, giving it a chance to be something better."

The Doctor smiled, feeling a surge of hope. "Exactly. This is the heart of balance: change. It's not about recreating perfection; it's about learning from what came before and allowing new life to find its own way."

The Death Moth's wings slowed, and its light began to dim as the last waves of energy settled into the landscape. The moth hovered for a moment, its eyes glowing faintly as it gazed down at the world it had just revitalized.

"LIFE WILL... BEGIN ANEW," it intoned softly. *"THE MEMO-RIES OF... THE PAST WILL... GUIDE THEM."*

The Doctor nodded, his expression thoughtful. "Yes, and we'll be here to help them. To guide them, so they don't fall into the same traps that brought them to ruin before."

The moth turned its gaze toward him, and for a moment, the Doctor felt the immense consciousness of the creature weighing on him—a consciousness that was ancient, vast, and filled with the knowledge of countless worlds. It was as if the moth was not just granting life but passing on the torch of responsibility to those who remained.

"BALANCE IS A... CONTINUOUS STRUGGLE," it murmured, its voice fading as it began to ascend. *"YOU... WILL GUIDE. WE WILL... WATCH."*

The Doctor watched as the Death Moth rose higher into the sky, its light growing fainter until it vanished into the clouds. The warmth it had left behind continued to spread, bringing life to the world below. Trees rustled in the gentle breeze, and the scent of fresh earth filled the air. It was a world reborn, not as it once was, but as something new and filled with potential.

Kelnar turned to the Doctor, his face radiant with hope. "We did it," he said, his voice trembling. "We've brought life back."

The Doctor smiled, though his eyes carried the weight of the journey still ahead. "Yes, we have. But this is just the beginning. The rebirth of worlds is only the first step. Now, we must guide them, help them remember the past and build a future that doesn't fall into the same patterns of destruction."

As they stood amidst the new growth, the Doctor felt a flicker of warmth in his hearts. The Death Moth had shown that it could be more than a force of devastation—it could be a guardian of renewal, of life. And with that revelation came a new hope for the universe.

It wasn't going to be easy. Balance was an ever-shifting state, a dance between chaos and harmony. But with the Death Moth as a keeper of memories and the Doctor as its guide, there was a chance that the worlds they touched could find a way to thrive.

"Come on, Kelnar," the Doctor said, turning toward the horizon. "We have much work to do. A world to nurture, lives to rebuild. The rebirth has begun, but the future depends on what we do next."

Together, they walked forward into the revitalized landscape, the echoes of the Death Moth's power lingering in the air. It was a new dawn, the start of a journey toward balance and growth. And with each step, the Doctor vowed to honor the memory of what had been lost by guiding what had now been given the chance to flourish.

Chapter 18: A New Threat Emerges

The sun was setting on the newly rejuvenated world, casting golden hues across the forest that had grown from the Death Moth's revitalizing energy. The Doctor stood in a clearing, his eyes taking in the sight of new life flourishing where only desolation had once reigned. Trees rustled in the breeze, rivers flowed with crystal clarity, and the air was filled with the chirping of small creatures beginning to explore their revitalized habitat.

Kelnar approached, a rare smile on his face as he marveled at the transformation around them. "It's beautiful, Doctor. You and the Death Moth... you've brought this world back to life."

The Doctor nodded, though his gaze remained fixed on the horizon. "Yes, we've given it a new beginning. But remember, Kelnar, this is only the start. Balance must be maintained, and that requires constant vigilance."

Kelnar's smile faded slightly as he sensed the Doctor's unease. "What's bothering you, Doctor? Everything seems peaceful now. The Daleks and Cybermen are gone, and the Death Moth is helping guide this rebirth."

The Doctor sighed, turning to face him. "That's precisely the problem. Peace is fragile, and there are always those who would seek to exploit it. The Death Moth's power is vast, almost beyond comprehension, and someone out there will inevitably try to harness it for their own ends." His expression grew dark, the shadow of an old memory flickering in his eyes. "I just have a feeling that... something—or rather, someone—is coming."

Before Kelnar could respond, a sudden gust of wind swept through the clearing, whipping up leaves and dust. The temperature dropped sharply, and the Doctor stiffened, sensing an unnatural disturbance in the air. His eyes narrowed, scanning the surroundings.

A low hum filled the air, accompanied by a rhythmic, wheezing groan that sent a shiver down the Doctor's spine. He recognized that sound all too well—it was the sound of a materializing TARDIS.

"No..." the Doctor whispered, his face paling. "It can't be."

Kelnar looked around, his eyes wide with confusion. "What is it, Doctor? What's happening?"

The Doctor grabbed his arm and pulled him back into the cover of the trees. "Hide!" he hissed. "Someone's coming, and they're not here for a friendly chat."

As they crouched behind the foliage, a dark-blue TARDIS material-ized in the center of the clearing. Its form was similar to the Doctor's own TARDIS but worn, scarred by the passage of time. The door creaked open, and from the shadowy interior emerged a figure draped in a long, tattered coat, his features partially obscured by the dim light.

The figure stepped forward, and as he moved into the light, the Doctor's eyes widened in recognition. The man was tall, his sharp eyes gleaming with a mixture of intelligence and malice. His face bore a faint, mocking smile that sent a chill down the Doctor's spine.

"Hello, Doctor," the figure called out, his voice smooth and drip-ping with condescension. "Did you really think you could hide from me in this forsaken corner of the universe?"

The Doctor straightened from his hiding place, stepping forward into the clearing. "Koschei," he said, his voice grim. "I should have known it was you."

The rogue Time Lord—better known to many as the Mas-ter—smirked, his eyes gleaming with an unsettling light. "Always the cautious one, Doctor. I must say, you've been busy, haven't you?" He gestured around at the rejuvenated landscape. "Bringing dead worlds back to life, playing the guardian of balance."

"What are you doing here?" the Doctor demanded, his eyes fixed on the Master. "This world has nothing to offer you. Leave now, before you do something you'll regret."

The Master chuckled, crossing his arms. "Oh, but you're wrong, old friend. This world has precisely what I seek: the power of the Death Moth. I've sensed it from across time and space, a force so vast that it could rewrite reality itself." His smile widened into something cruel. "And I intend to control it."

The Doctor's heart skipped a beat, and he clenched his fists. "You can't control the Death Moth," he said, his voice filled with urgency. "It's not just a force; it's a consciousness bound to the balance of the universe. If you try to harness it, you'll provoke a reaction that could devastate not just this world, but countless others."

The Master raised an eyebrow, his expression turning mockingly thoughtful. "Yes, I've read the legends," he replied, waving a dismissive hand. "A cosmic entity that guards the balance, a keeper of memories. All very poetic, Doctor. But you and I both know that legends are often just a matter of perspective."

He began to circle the clearing, his eyes gleaming as he spoke. "Think of it, Doctor: the power to reshape reality, to bend the cosmos to one's will. The Death Moth's energy is pure, unfiltered by the constraints of time or morality. In the right hands—my hands—it could create a new order, one where balance is defined by *me*."

"Or it could destroy you," the Doctor retorted, his voice steady but laced with anger. "You're meddling with forces beyond even a Time Lord's comprehension. The moth isn't a tool; it's a guardian. If you try to seize its power, it will annihilate you."

The Master stopped, turning to face him with a smile that was equal parts madness and cunning. "Perhaps," he conceded, his tone light. "But then, isn't that what makes it worth the risk? You see, Doctor, you're content to be a mere caretaker, nurturing these worlds back to life. But I... I aim higher. I seek to become a god."

The Doctor stepped forward, his eyes blazing. "You seek destruction, and you'll find it," he said, his voice like iron. "I won't let you twist the moth's power to serve your delusions of grandeur."

The Master tilted his head, studying the Doctor with a predatory gaze. "Won't let me?" he echoed, his voice dripping with amusement. "Oh, Doctor, you seem to forget: I have the means to do as I please."

He reached into his coat, producing a small, intricate device that emitted a faint, rhythmic pulse. The Doctor's eyes widened as he recognized the object—a temporal disruptor, designed to pierce through protective fields and channel raw energy.

"You plan to trap the moth with that?" the Doctor asked incredulously, his mind racing. "You're madder than I thought."

The Master's smile widened. "Not trap, Doctor. Merge. The disruptor will allow me to interface directly with the moth's essence, to bind its power to my will."

"No!" the Doctor shouted, raising his sonic screwdriver. "I won't let you do this!"

In a flash, the Master flicked his wrist, and the disruptor emitted a pulse that sent the Doctor stumbling back, his body momentarily paralyzed by the shockwave. "You always were so predictable, Doctor," the Master sneered. "Always rushing in, thinking you can stop the inevitable."

He turned toward the sky, raising the disruptor high. "Death Moth!" he called out, his voice echoing through the air. "Hear me! I summon you! Come forth and submit to my command!"

The air grew frigid, and a deep, resonant hum filled the clearing. The Doctor struggled to his feet, his eyes widening as the familiar glow began to appear above them. The Death Moth descended, its wings unfurling with an intensity that caused the very ground to tremble.

The Doctor could feel the moth's presence pressing into his mind, a wave of cold, ancient power that filled the air with an almost unbearable tension. It hovered before the Master, its eyes blazing with a light that was both furious and wary.

The Master raised the disruptor, grinning madly. "Yes," he hissed. "Yes, come to me. You are mine to command."

The moth's eyes flared, and a surge of energy erupted from its form, crashing into the disruptor. The device crackled, sparks flying as it absorbed the moth's power. The Master staggered, his face twisted in a mix of triumph and strain as he fought to channel the force.

But the moth did not yield. It lashed out again, this time sending a shockwave of dark energy that struck the Master, knocking him to the ground. The disruptor fell from his grasp, sparking violently as it rolled away.

The Doctor stepped forward, his sonic screwdriver in hand. "You've lost, Koschei!" he shouted. "You can't control it. The moth won't be bound to your will!"

The Master snarled, struggling to rise. "No... it's not over," he gasped, reaching out toward the disruptor.

But before he could grasp it, the moth's eyes blazed once more, and a tendril of light shot forth, enveloping the device. With a sound like shattering glass, the disruptor disintegrated, its pieces scattering into dust.

The Doctor felt the air grow still, the tension lifting as the moth hovered silently above them. It turned its gaze to the Doctor, its eyes glowing with a light that spoke of understanding and resolve.

"BALANCE MUST... BE MAINTAINED," it intoned softly. *"THOSE WHO SEEK... TO DOMINATE WILL... BE CORRECTED."*

The Doctor nodded, his expression somber. "Yes," he agreed. "But let's not destroy him. He's a fool, yes, but even fools can learn."

The moth's wings folded slightly, its eyes dimming. *"VERY WELL,"* it murmured. *"HE WILL BE... SPARED, BUT NOT... LEFT UNWATCHED."*

With that, the moth began to ascend, its form shimmering as it vanished into the sky. The Doctor turned to the Master, who lay on the ground, his face contorted with rage and humiliation.

"You never learn, do you?" the Doctor said quietly, approaching him. "You seek power, but you don't understand that true strength lies in balance, in guidance, not domination."

The Master glared at him, his eyes burning with defiance. "Balance," he spat. "A weak man's excuse for cowardice."

The Doctor sighed, shaking his head. "No, Koschei. It's not weakness. It's wisdom. And until you learn that, you'll keep failing."

He turned away, his gaze drifting toward the horizon. "Come on, Kelnar," he called. "We have a world to guide, and now, an old enemy to watch."

As they walked away, the Doctor couldn't help but glance back at the Master. He knew that the rogue Time Lord would not give up easily. This was only the beginning of a new struggle, one that would test his resolve to maintain balance in the face of those who sought to upend it.

But with the Death Moth now an ally—an entity that understood the necessity of growth and renewal—there was hope. And the Doctor, ever the guardian, would continue to guide the universe toward a future where balance was not enforced through power, but through wisdom and harmony.

Chapter 19: The Time Lord's Plan

The night in the shadow world was unnaturally quiet. The stars above gleamed faintly, barely piercing through the canopy of new growth that had spread across the land. Despite the world's apparent rebirth, an underlying tension thickened the air. The Doctor stood outside the newly grown forest, his gaze fixed on the horizon where the Master's TARDIS had materialized earlier. The battle was far from over. He knew the Master was planning something far more catastrophic than a simple power grab.

Behind him, Kelnar approached cautiously, his face etched with concern. "Doctor, what do we do now? The Master won't just give up. He's here for the Death Moth, and he'll stop at nothing."

The Doctor sighed, running a hand through his hair. "You're right," he said grimly. "The Master is far too cunning and tenacious to let a setback deter him. He's tasted the power of the moth, and now he'll want to control it entirely. But it's not just about control this time, Kelnar. There's something more at stake."

"What do you mean?" Kelnar asked, his eyes widening.

The Doctor turned to face him, his expression hardening. "The Master has always been obsessed with rewriting the universe in his image. The moth's power is not limited to simple destruction or renewal; it's a force that can interact with the very fabric of time itself. If the Master succeeds in binding the Death Moth's energy to his will, he could potentially rewrite history, erasing every victory, every triumph, every balance I've ever fought to maintain."

Kelnar paled. "He... he would erase everything?"

The Doctor nodded solemnly. "Yes. Not just my victories, but every milestone that keeps the universe from descending into chaos. He wants to bring the cosmos to a state of anarchy, where he alone holds sway over time. And with the Death Moth's power, he might actually be able to do it."

A soft breeze rustled through the trees, a stark contrast to the dark conversation. The Doctor's mind raced, piecing together the fragments of the Master's plan. The moth was a cosmic entity tied to the natural cycles of existence—birth, death, and rebirth. If the Master were to hijack that power, he could bend those cycles to suit his twisted designs.

The Doctor's eyes narrowed as he looked at the stars. "I need to confront him," he murmured, his voice low. "Find out how he intends to use the moth's power. If I can understand his plan, I might find a way to stop him without forcing the moth into a defensive reaction."

Kelnar stepped forward, worry etched on his face. "But Doctor, the Master is dangerous. If you go to him now, he could trap you, or worse..."

The Doctor placed a reassuring hand on Kelnar's shoulder. "I know the risks," he said, a faint, almost bitter smile on his lips. "But this is the only way. I need to engage him directly. Keep watch here; if anything happens, use the temple's carvings to call on the Death Moth."

With that, the Doctor turned and began to walk toward the clearing where the Master's TARDIS had appeared. As he approached, the familiar hum of the temporal field filled the air, a reminder of the delicate balance they were all teetering on.

The Master was already waiting for him, standing in front of his TARDIS with an expression of casual disdain. His arms were crossed over his chest, and the corners of his mouth curled into a mocking smile as the Doctor approached.

"Ah, Doctor," the Master drawled, his eyes glinting with malice. "I knew you'd come. You can't resist a confrontation, can you? Always the noble defender, always the fool."

"Spare me the theatrics, Koschei," the Doctor snapped, his voice cold. "I know you're planning something far worse than merely seizing the moth's power. You want to rewrite the universe, don't you? Erase every victory, every balance, and bring chaos to the cosmos."

The Master's smile widened, his eyes gleaming with an unhinged light. "Bravo, Doctor," he purred. "You've pieced it together. Yes, that is precisely my plan. With the Death Moth's energy, I can rewrite time itself. Erase all your pitiful victories, wipe out the pointless order you've tried so hard to maintain. I will create a universe where I am the sole arbiter of time, chaos, and balance."

The Doctor felt a chill run down his spine. "You're mad," he said, his voice a mix of horror and anger. "You'd plunge the entire cosmos into a state of entropy. The moth's power is tied to the natural cycles of existence. If you break that cycle, you risk tearing apart the very fabric of reality."

The Master laughed, a sharp, almost musical sound that echoed through the clearing. "Oh, Doctor, you're so limited in your thinking. Tearing apart reality is the whole point! The universe is too rigid, too defined by rules and structures. By harnessing the moth's power, I can unravel those constraints. A new dawn of chaos, one that I control."

The Doctor's eyes narrowed, his mind racing to find a way to counter this twisted plan. "You'll never control it," he said, his voice low and dangerous. "The Death Moth isn't just a force of energy—it's a consciousness bound to balance. If you try to bend it to your will, it will fight back, and the consequences will be catastrophic."

The Master shrugged, his smile never faltering. "That's the beauty of it, Doctor. Catastrophe is merely the first step toward creation. The moth's consciousness is powerful, yes, but it's not invincible. I've studied it, learned how to weaken its resolve, how to channel its energy through temporal conduits. Once I bind it to my TARDIS, I'll be able to reshape time as I see fit."

The Doctor clenched his fists, feeling the rising urge to lash out. "You won't succeed," he growled. "I won't let you. I'll stop you, even if it means confronting the moth directly to break your hold on it."

The Master's eyes flashed with anger, his demeanor shifting from mocking amusement to cold fury. "You always have to make things difficult, don't you?" he hissed. "Very well, Doctor. If you want to play the hero, then try to stop me."

He raised his hand, revealing a sleek, metallic device covered in arcane symbols and circuitry. The Doctor recognized it immediately—a temporal amplifier, designed to tap into the moth's energy and project it through the Master's TARDIS.

"I'll bind the moth's power here," the Master continued, his voice filled with triumph. "And then, I will rewrite history, starting with your precious Earth. I'll erase every victory, every act of defiance, and replace them with my own narrative."

The Doctor's hearts pounded in his chest. He needed to act quickly, to find a way to disrupt the amplifier and break the Master's connection to the Death Moth. But he also needed to avoid provoking the moth into a destructive reaction. It was a delicate balance, and he was running out of time.

"Think, think, think," he muttered to himself, glancing at the device in the Master's hand. He needed a plan, a way to sever the temporal link without causing a catastrophic backlash.

The Master watched him with a smug grin. "Having trouble, Doctor?" he taunted. "You've always been good at finding solutions, but this time, you're out of your depth. The Death Moth is beyond even your control."

The Doctor suddenly froze, his eyes widening as an idea struck him. Control. That was the key. The Master was trying to exert control over a force that inherently resisted domination. If he could introduce enough chaos into the temporal amplifier, it might cause a feedback loop, disrupting the Master's connection and freeing the moth.

He raised his sonic screwdriver, his eyes locking onto the amplifier. "You're right, Master," he said, his voice calm but edged with determination. "The moth is beyond control. But that doesn't mean I can't introduce a little... chaos of my own."

Before the Master could react, the Doctor activated the sonic screwdriver, sending a pulse of energy toward the amplifier. The device sparked and crackled, its circuitry flashing erratically as the temporal field around it began to destabilize.

"What have you done?" the Master snarled, clutching the amplifier as it buzzed and hissed in his grip. "You're disrupting the temporal harmonics!"

"That's the idea," the Doctor replied, his eyes blazing. "You wanted chaos, Master? Here it is!"

The amplifier emitted a high-pitched whine, and a shockwave of temporal energy erupted from it, blasting both the Doctor and the Master off their feet. The air shimmered with erratic currents of time, warping the space around them.

The Master struggled to his feet, his face twisted with rage. "You fool!" he screamed. "You've ruined everything!"

The Doctor slowly stood, clutching his sonic screwdriver as he steadied himself. "Not ruined," he corrected, his voice firm. "Redirected. The Death Moth isn't your puppet, and it never will be."

Above them, the sky darkened as the Death Moth descended, its wings beating furiously. Its eyes glowed with an intense light, casting twin beams that swept across the clearing. The temporal disturbance around the amplifier began to stabilize, pulled into the moth's energy field as it hovered over the scene.

The Master's eyes widened in horror. "No!" he shrieked, backing away. "I can still control it!"

The Doctor stepped forward, his gaze fixed on the moth. "No, you can't," he said quietly. "The moth belongs to the universe, to the balance it maintains. Not to you. Never to you."

The Death Moth turned its gaze toward the Master, its eyes glowing brighter. *"YOU SOUGHT TO... DOMINATE TIME,"* it intoned, its voice echoing through the air like a judge passing sentence. *"BALANCE WILL NOT BE... MANIPULATED."*

The Master stumbled back, his face pale. "You can't... no..." he gasped.

The moth raised its wings, and a wave of energy surged forth, enveloping the Master in a cocoon of light. He screamed, thrashing against the force, but it held firm, lifting him off the ground.

The Doctor watched, his expression a mixture of pity and resolve. "You brought this on yourself, Koschei," he said softly. "You can't force balance to bend to your will. It's time you learned that."

The light around the Master intensified, and with a final, anguished scream, he vanished, drawn into the moth's energy. The air grew still, the temporal currents dissipating as the moth lowered itself to the ground.

The Doctor approached, his hearts heavy. "You've spared him, haven't you?" he asked, sensing the moth's intent.

"HE IS... CONTAINED," the moth replied. *"HIS THREAT IS... NEUTRALIZED, BUT HE WILL... REMAIN UNDER WATCH."*

The Doctor nodded, relief mingling with exhaustion. "Thank you," he said quietly. "Now, we can continue our work. The universe still needs balance, and there's so much left to do."

The Death Moth hovered silently for a moment, its eyes gleaming with an understanding that transcended words. Then, with a final, gentle sweep of its wings, it ascended into the sky, leaving behind a sense of calm and renewal.

The Doctor turned back to Kelnar, who emerged cautiously from the trees, his eyes wide with awe. "Is... is it over?" Kelnar asked, his voice trembling.

The Doctor nodded, a faint smile on his lips. "For now, yes. The Master's plan has been thwarted, and the moth remains free to guide, not to dominate. But our work isn't finished. Balance is an ongoing journey, one that we must continue to walk."

As they stood in the clearing, the stars above shone a little brighter, a reminder that in the vast expanse of the universe, the struggle for balance was eternal. And as long as the Doctor was there to guide, there was hope that chaos would not prevail.

Chapter 20: The Battle for Time

The air crackled with tension in the clearing, where the echoes of the previous confrontation still lingered like a haunting melody. The stars above seemed to pulse with an unnatural energy, responding to the temporal distortions emanating from the Master's TARDIS. The Doctor knew the reprieve was temporary; the Master would find a way back, more determined and dangerous than before. He wasn't wrong.

A low, rhythmic hum filled the air, and the Doctor turned sharply toward the sound. The Master's TARDIS began to shimmer, its form twisting and warping, a distortion in the fabric of reality itself. With a blinding flash, the Master materialized, his eyes burning with an intensity that sent a chill down the Doctor's spine.

"Did you really think it would be that easy, Doctor?" the Master sneered, stepping out from the twisted vortex. His presence warped the air around him, bending the shadows into unnatural shapes. In his hand, he clutched the temporal amplifier, its circuitry now buzzing with a malevolent energy.

The Doctor stepped forward, his expression grim. "Give it up, Koschei," he called out. "Your plan is doomed. The Death Moth isn't a weapon for you to wield. It's a guardian, a force of balance. If you try to force it, you'll destroy yourself—and possibly everything else in the process."

The Master's eyes narrowed, his lips curling into a cruel smile. "Ah, Doctor, always the voice of reason," he taunted. "But reason has no place in the face of power. I've seen what the moth can do, the power it holds. And now, I'll bend that power to rewrite reality itself."

Without warning, the Master raised the amplifier, sending a pulse of dark energy hurtling toward the Doctor. The ground shook as the blast expanded, warping space around it into a vortex of shimmering light and shadow. The Doctor stumbled back, narrowly avoiding the swirling energy that lashed out like tendrils seeking to ensnare him.

"You're meddling with forces beyond even your comprehension, Koschei!" the Doctor shouted, his voice strained as he raised his sonic screwdriver. "This isn't a simple power struggle; you're tampering with the fabric of time itself!"

The Master's laughter rang out, cold and mocking. "Oh, I know exactly what I'm doing," he snarled. "And it's glorious! I'm not just seizing power—I'm reshaping history. Every victory you've ever claimed, every balance you've maintained—it will all be erased, rewritten in my image."

The Doctor gritted his teeth, feeling the gravity of the situation weigh down on him. The Master had gone beyond mere conquest; he was attempting to disrupt the very essence of time. The Death Moth's energy, if fully harnessed, could rewrite the past, unmake the present, and alter the future. He couldn't let that happen.

"I won't let you do this!" the Doctor shouted, his eyes blazing with determination. "You think you can control the moth, but it will resist you. And if you push it too far, it will retaliate in ways you can't even begin to comprehend!"

The Master's smile widened, and he activated the amplifier once more. "That's the beauty of it, Doctor," he hissed. "I'm not trying to control it—I'm becoming *one* with it. Once I merge with its essence, I will *be* the balance, the arbiter of time itself."

The ground beneath them split open as the amplifier's energy surged upward, creating a vortex of swirling temporal currents. The air around them shimmered, and the sky above darkened, as if the stars themselves were recoiling from the unnatural disturbance. The Doctor felt the pull of the vortex, a force that tugged at the edges of his consciousness, threatening to drag him into the maelstrom.

He glanced around desperately, searching for any sign of the Death Moth. It was their only chance; the moth had to intervene, had to stop the Master before he could merge with its power. But would it come?

Then, from the depths of the vortex, a faint glow appeared, growing brighter and more intense with every passing second. The Doctor's heart leaped as he recognized the ethereal light—it was the Death Moth, drawn by the disturbance, torn between its cosmic purpose and its connection with the Doctor.

The moth descended, its wings unfurling with a brilliance that cast shadows across the clearing. Its eyes blazed, twin stars in the darkening sky, as it hovered between the Doctor and the Master, its form pulsating with the energy of the universe itself.

The Master's eyes gleamed with triumph. "Yes!" he cried, raising the amplifier toward the moth. "Come to me! You are mine to command, to merge with!"

The Doctor stepped forward, his voice trembling with urgency. "Death Moth, listen to me!" he shouted. "You are a guardian of balance, a keeper of memories! Don't let him twist your purpose into chaos!"

The moth hesitated, its form rippling with an internal conflict. The Doctor could sense its struggle—the pull between its ancient duty to correct imbalances and the temptation of merging with the Master's will, which promised an escape from the endless cycles of birth, death, and rebirth.

The Master laughed, his voice a harsh cackle that echoed through the vortex. "You see, Doctor? Even the moth is torn! It knows that balance is an illusion, a lie that you've clung to for far too long!"

"Balance isn't an illusion!" the Doctor retorted, his eyes locking onto the moth's gaze. "It's a choice. It's the willingness to guide the universe, not control it! You have a purpose, Death Moth, and that purpose is not to become a weapon in the hands of a madman."

The moth's eyes flickered, its wings beating faster as it seemed to draw in on itself. The vortex around them grew unstable, the temporal currents swirling wildly as the moth wrestled with the pull of the Master's amplifier.

Sensing the moth's hesitation, the Master pressed forward, his face alight with manic glee. "Join me!" he commanded, his voice resonating with an unnatural power. "Together, we will rewrite the cosmos, remake time in our image! No more balance, no more endless cycles—only power!"

The Doctor gritted his teeth, feeling the pressure of the temporal currents closing in around him. He had to reach the moth, had to make it see that it had the power to choose its own path.

"Death Moth!" he cried out, his voice carrying through the vortex. "Listen to me! You've seen the cycles of history, the rise and fall of worlds. You've preserved memories, guided life toward renewal. That's your true purpose—not to serve those who would twist reality for their own ends!"

The moth paused, its wings folding inward as it hovered between the two Time Lords. The air grew thick with anticipation, the energy in the clearing reaching a fever pitch. The Doctor held his breath, his hearts pounding as he waited for the moth's decision.

Then, slowly, the moth began to glow, its light intensifying until it outshone the darkness of the vortex. Its wings unfurled, casting beams of radiant energy that swept across the landscape. The air around it crackled with power, a power that spoke of both destruction and creation, of endings and beginnings.

The Master's eyes widened in horror as the moth turned its gaze toward him. "No... NO!" he screamed, raising the amplifier in a desperate attempt to channel the moth's energy.

But the moth moved with a speed and grace that defied comprehension. It lashed out, sending a wave of light that struck the amplifier, shattering it into fragments. The device exploded in a burst of temporal energy, sending the Master flying backward into the vortex.

The Doctor felt the shockwave ripple through the air, and he raised his arms to shield himself as the currents around them twisted and buckled. The vortex collapsed inward, dragging the Master into its depths. He screamed, his voice echoing through the rift as he was swallowed by the temporal storm.

"No!" he howled, his voice fading into the void. "This isn't over, Doctor! You haven't seen the last of me!"

With a final burst of light, the vortex imploded, leaving only the Death Moth hovering above the clearing, its wings beating slowly. The air grew still, the tension dissipating as the stars above returned to their normal brilliance.

The Doctor lowered his arms, breathing heavily as he looked up at the moth. "You did it," he murmured, his voice filled with both awe and relief. "You chose balance over chaos."

The moth descended, its eyes glowing softly as it regarded the Doctor. *"BALANCE IS... A CHOICE,"* it intoned, its voice echoing through the stillness. *"WE ARE... NOT A TOOL OF... DOMINATION."*

The Doctor nodded, his expression one of quiet understanding. "No, you're not," he agreed. "You're a guardian, a guide for the universe. And you've proven today that your purpose goes beyond destruction. It's about preserving the potential for renewal, for growth."

The moth's form shimmered, its light dimming slightly as it began to ascend into the sky. *"WE WILL... WATCH,"* it murmured. *"BALANCE MUST BE... MAINTAINED."*

The Doctor watched as the moth disappeared into the stars, leaving behind a sense of calm and a renewed hope for the future. He turned to Kelnar, who emerged from the cover of the trees, his eyes wide with awe.

"Is it... over?" Kelnar asked, his voice trembling.

The Doctor nodded, though his expression remained solemn. "For now, yes. The Master has been defeated, and the moth has chosen to remain a guardian, not a tool of chaos." He took a deep breath, letting the tension seep out of his body. "But balance is an ongoing struggle, and the battle for time will always be just beyond the horizon."

Kelnar looked at him, a flicker of concern in his eyes. "And the Master? Will he come back?"

The Doctor's gaze drifted to the spot where the vortex had collapsed. "The Master always finds a way," he admitted. "But we'll be ready. As long as the Death Moth continues to choose its purpose, and as long as we remain vigilant, there's hope."

He turned toward the horizon, where the first light of dawn was beginning to break. "Come on, Kelnar," he said, his voice resolute. "There's a universe out there that needs our guidance. Let's make sure that balance is something we continue to nurture, one step at a time."

With that, they began their journey forward, leaving behind the scars of the battle for time and moving toward the promise of renewal and growth. The cosmos stretched out before them, vast and full of potential, and the Doctor knew that while the struggle for balance was never-ending, it was a struggle worth fighting.

Chapter 21: A Sacrifice

The morning light of the newly revitalized world brought a fleeting sense of peace. Birds chirped in the trees, and the air was filled with the earthy scent of fresh growth. However, beneath this serene surface, a storm brewed within the Doctor's mind. He stood at the edge of a cliff, overlooking a valley that had once been a barren wasteland but now teemed with life. The battle with the Master had been won, but the price of maintaining that victory loomed heavy on his hearts.

Behind him, Kelnar approached cautiously, noticing the Doctor's solemn demeanor. "Doctor," he began, his voice quiet but filled with concern. "You did it. You stopped the Master. The Death Moth chose to protect the balance."

The Doctor nodded, his gaze fixed on the horizon. "Yes," he said softly. "The Master's plan was thwarted, and the moth has proven itself as a guardian. But this isn't over, Kelnar."

Kelnar frowned, stepping closer. "What do you mean? The Master is gone, at least for now. We can focus on rebuilding, on guiding this world toward a better future."

The Doctor turned to face him, and Kelnar saw the weight of sorrow etched in his eyes. "I wish it were that simple," the Doctor replied. "The Master may be gone, but he has left his mark. His tampering with the Death Moth's essence has upset the balance in ways I didn't anticipate. The universe itself is now... unraveling."

Kelnar blinked, his face pale. "Unraveling? How?"

The Doctor sighed, running a hand through his hair as he searched for the right words. "The moth's power is connected to the cycles of time and existence. When the Master tried to merge with its energy, he created a disturbance that's rippling through the fabric of reality. The cosmos is destabilizing, and it's only a matter of time before the effects become catastrophic."

He paused, looking down at the ground as he wrestled with the truth he'd been avoiding. "The only way to restore the balance," he continued slowly, "is to allow the Death Moth to return to its original purpose: a cosmic guardian that acts as a reset mechanism for worlds teetering on the edge of destruction."

Kelnar's eyes widened in horror. "You mean... you have to let it destroy everything again?"

The Doctor shook his head. "Not everything," he replied, his voice barely a whisper. "But enough to reset the balance, to contain the chaos that the Master unleashed. And it means letting the moth go back to the shadow world, where it can once more become a force that exists outside the influence of any individual."

Kelnar stumbled back, shock and disbelief clouding his features. "But... but you've worked so hard to restore this world! You've guided the moth toward renewal, toward becoming something more than a force of destruction!"

A pang of pain shot through the Doctor's hearts as he heard the truth in Kelnar's words. "I know," he murmured, his voice cracking slightly. "But some battles can't be won without a cost. This universe, this balance, demands a sacrifice. The moth's new path was inspiring, but the Master's interference has corrupted the balance. The moth must return to its role as a cosmic resetter, at least for now."

Kelnar stared at him, his eyes brimming with desperation. "You're going to say goodbye to it, aren't you? After everything?"

The Doctor nodded, a lump forming in his throat. "Yes," he said hoarsely. "It's the only way to save this world and the countless others that depend on the balance the moth maintains."

Before Kelnar could respond, a faint hum filled the air, growing louder with each passing moment. The sky above them darkened, and a familiar glow began to form in the clouds. The Doctor felt the air grow cold, and he turned to face the approaching light.

The Death Moth descended, its wings beating slowly, casting long shadows across the landscape. Its eyes glowed with a light that held both the wisdom of ages and a quiet, ancient sorrow. The Doctor stepped forward, feeling the gravity of the moment settle over him like a heavy cloak.

"You heard," the Doctor said, his voice soft but steady. "You felt the disturbance the Master caused."

The moth hovered silently for a moment, its wings stirring the air with a faint, rhythmic hum. *"BALANCE HAS BEEN... DISTURBED,"* it intoned, its voice resonating like the tolling of a distant bell. *"THE CYCLES OF TIME AND... EXISTENCE REQUIRE RESETTING."*

The Doctor nodded, swallowing the lump in his throat. "I know," he replied. "And I know what that means for you. Returning to your purpose, resetting the worlds that have fallen into imbalance."

The moth's eyes flickered, and its wings folded slightly as it lowered itself to meet the Doctor's gaze. *"WE HAVE LEARNED... FROM YOU,"* it murmured. *"RENEWAL, GROWTH... ARE POSSIBILITIES. BUT SOME IMBALANCES... REQUIRE CORRECTION THROUGH... ENDINGS."*

The Doctor felt a wave of anguish wash over him, and he struggled to keep his voice steady. "Yes," he said quietly. "But it doesn't mean you're just a destroyer. It means you're the guardian of balance, and sometimes that requires letting go of what we've built to protect the greater whole."

He took a deep breath, his eyes locking onto the moth's glowing gaze. "I wish... I wish it didn't have to be this way," he admitted, his voice breaking slightly. "But I can't be the one to dictate the balance of the universe. You're the keeper of that, and I have to let you fulfill your destiny."

The moth hovered in silence, its wings beating gently as if contemplating the Doctor's words. *"THE UNIVERSE IS... A CYCLE,"* it intoned softly. *"TO MAINTAIN BALANCE, SOME MUST... FALL SO THAT OTHERS MAY... RISE."*

The Doctor nodded, feeling a tear slip down his cheek. "Then it's time," he whispered. "Go back to the shadow world, and fulfill your purpose. I'll find a way to guide the universe forward, even if it means starting from the beginning."

Kelnar stepped forward, his voice trembling. "Doctor, there must be another way!"

The Doctor turned to him, his face drawn with grief. "If there was, I would take it," he said softly. "But this is the price we must pay to restore what the Master tried to destroy. Balance demands a sacrifice, and this time, it's the path we've tried to create with the moth."

The Death Moth began to ascend, its wings spreading wide as its glow intensified. The ground beneath it trembled, and the air filled with a hum that resonated through the landscape. The Doctor stepped back, his eyes fixed on the creature that had become his ally, his guide.

"WE WILL... RETURN TO THE... SHADOW WORLD," the moth intoned, its voice echoing through the air like the whispers of time itself. *"AND IN DOING SO, WE WILL... RESET THE IMBALANCE. THE WORLDS WILL... REMEMBER."*

The Doctor felt a surge of bittersweet pride. "They will remember," he agreed, his voice barely audible. "And they'll grow. Because that's the legacy we leave behind: the memory of what was, guiding what will be."

The moth hovered for a moment longer, its light washing over the Doctor and Kelnar like a final embrace. Then, with a sweep of its wings, it began to rise, its form shimmering as it ascended into the sky. The clouds parted to reveal a swirling vortex of light and shadow—the entrance to the shadow world, where the moth would resume its cosmic role.

As the moth disappeared into the vortex, the Doctor felt a sharp pang in his hearts. He had hoped to guide the moth toward a new path, a role beyond destruction. But he knew that sometimes, the hardest choices were the ones that ensured the survival of the greater whole.

Kelnar watched, tears streaming down his face. "Doctor... I'm so sorry."

The Doctor placed a hand on Kelnar's shoulder, offering a faint, sad smile. "So am I," he replied. "But this isn't the end. The Death Moth returns to its duty, yes, but it carries with it the lessons we've shared. It's not just a force of annihilation—it's a guardian that remembers, that preserves the knowledge of what has been lost. That's what will guide us forward."

He turned away from the cliff, his eyes scanning the horizon where new life was already beginning to emerge. "Come on," he said quietly. "We have a lot of work to do. The universe needs balance, and even without the moth at our side, we have to keep striving to maintain it."

Kelnar nodded, though his face remained etched with sorrow. "Where do we start?"

The Doctor took a deep breath, steeling himself. "We start by honoring the memory of what was sacrificed today," he said firmly. "We guide the new life that rises from this, teach it the value of balance, of growth. And we do it knowing that somewhere out there, the Death Moth watches, ensuring that we never forget the lessons of the past."

As they walked away from the cliff, the sky slowly began to brighten, the first rays of sunlight piercing through the darkness. The Doctor knew the path ahead would be fraught with challenges, that the struggle for balance would never truly end. But he also knew that with every ending came the potential for a new beginning.

And as long as he carried the memory of the Death Moth within him, he would continue to fight for a universe that could rise, learn, and grow—even in the face of sacrifice.

Chapter 22: The End of the Daleks

The morning sun cast long shadows over the valley, a bittersweet reminder of the rebirth and loss that had just transpired. The Death Moth had returned to the shadow world, fulfilling its role in restoring cosmic balance. The universe felt stable, but the Doctor knew his task was far from over. There was still a dark presence lingering in the cosmos—the last remnants of the Daleks, hiding, rebuilding, scheming for their next chance at domination.

The Doctor stood at the edge of a vast field, his gaze fixed on the horizon. In his hand, he held the sonic screwdriver, absentmindedly twirling it as he mulled over the memories of his encounters with the Death Moth. In those encounters, he had glimpsed something more—a way to finally bring an end to the Daleks' ceaseless cycle of destruction.

Kelnar approached cautiously, his face still etched with the sorrow of recent events. "Doctor, the Death Moth is gone," he said quietly. "The balance is being restored, but... you're still troubled, aren't you?"

The Doctor turned, his eyes reflecting both determination and an underlying sorrow. "Yes, Kelnar," he replied. "The Death Moth has returned to its cosmic duties, but there remains a stain on this universe that needs to be wiped clean. The Daleks. They are relentless, surviving defeat after defeat, always crawling back to spread death and chaos."

Kelnar nodded, his face grim. "But what can we do? They've survived everything, even when we thought they were destroyed."

The Doctor slipped the sonic screwdriver into his pocket and straightened, a glint of resolve in his eyes. "I've learned something from the Death Moth," he began, his voice steady. "A way to ensure they never return, a way to erase their presence from the cosmic cycle once and for all. It won't be easy, and it will require a type of intervention that even I am hesitant to employ. But it's the only way."

Kelnar's eyes widened. "What are you saying, Doctor?"

The Doctor exhaled slowly, turning to face him. "The Daleks are creatures of pure destruction, driven by their insatiable desire for conquest. To stop them permanently, I need to locate their last surviving nests and utilize a form of energy that the Death Moth revealed to me—an energy that severs a being from the cycle of existence, removing its essence from the fabric of time."

Kelnar blinked in shock. "You're talking about... erasing them from time itself?"

"Yes," the Doctor admitted, his voice barely above a whisper. "The Death Moth's power was not just about destruction or renewal; it was about maintaining a balance. When it eradicated the Daleks before, it imprinted the memory of that act into the universe's consciousness, ensuring that the event remained a lesson in cosmic history. I can use a fragment of that power—through the knowledge it shared with me—to end the Daleks in such a way that they'll never rise again."

Kelnar stared at him, a mixture of awe and fear in his eyes. "But, Doctor, isn't that... dangerous? Tampering with time to erase an entire species?"

The Doctor sighed, his gaze hardening as he turned toward the horizon. "Yes, it's dangerous," he conceded. "But it's a risk that must be taken. The Daleks have threatened the balance of the universe for far too long. They are an aberration, a disease that must be eradicated to ensure that life can continue to grow and evolve. This is the only way to guarantee they never return."

Kelnar hesitated before speaking again. "How do you plan to do it?"

The Doctor's eyes narrowed, his mind racing through the steps of his plan. "We start by locating their last stronghold. The Death Moth left traces of their existence imprinted on this world, a sort of cosmic footprint. I can track it to find where the remnants of the Dalek Empire are hiding. Once we find them, I'll use the knowledge the moth imparted to disrupt their presence within the time stream."

He pulled out the sonic screwdriver and adjusted its settings, causing it to emit a soft hum that resonated with the energy around them. The air seemed to shimmer, responding to the screwdriver's vibrations as the Doctor began to search for the Dalek traces.

"Ah, there it is," he murmured, his eyes flickering with recognition. "A faint temporal distortion, emanating from the northeast. They've holed themselves up in a cavern system, hoping to rebuild their strength."

Kelnar swallowed hard. "So, what now?"

The Doctor pocketed the screwdriver, his face set with grim determination. "Now, we go to them. And we end this, once and for all."

The journey to the Dalek nest was fraught with tension. The caverns were dark and winding, the walls slick with an unnatural substance that glistened under the faint light of the Doctor's torch. As they descended deeper into the maze-like structure, the air grew colder, laced with the metallic scent of machinery and decay.

"They're here," the Doctor whispered, motioning for Kelnar to stay close. "I can sense their energy. They've been building, preparing for their return."

A distant, mechanical hum filled the caverns, followed by the unmistakable sound of grinding metal. The Doctor halted, listening intently. Then, from the shadows ahead, a Dalek glided into view, its eyestalk swiveling toward them.

"INTRUDERS DETECTED!" it screeched, its voice echoing off the cavern walls. "EXTERMINATE! EXTERMINATE!"

The Doctor raised his hands, his expression calm. "Not today," he said quietly, pulling out his sonic screwdriver. With a swift flick, he emitted a pulse that disabled the Dalek's weapon system, leaving it thrashing helplessly in place.

"YOU... WILL NOT... STOP US!" the Dalek rasped, its voice crackling with fury. "THE DALEK EMPIRE WILL... RISE AGAIN!"

The Doctor stepped forward, his eyes cold as steel. "No," he said firmly. "You won't."

He turned to Kelnar. "Stay back," he instructed. "I need to be close to the core of their nest to do this."

Kelnar nodded, retreating as the Doctor moved deeper into the cavern. More Daleks appeared, their metallic bodies glinting in the dim light. The Doctor moved swiftly, using the sonic screwdriver to disable them one by one until he reached the heart of the nest—a vast chamber filled with rows of dormant Daleks, their shells pulsing with a sickly yellow light.

The Doctor stepped into the center of the room, pulling out a small, crystalline shard from his pocket. The shard was a remnant of the Death Moth's power, left behind as a fragment of its cosmic energy. It glowed faintly, resonating with the temporal energy that filled the chamber.

"This is it," the Doctor muttered to himself. "The end of the Daleks."

He raised the shard, channeling the energy through his sonic screwdriver. A beam of light shot out, striking the walls of the chamber. The air vibrated with a deep hum as the energy expanded, spreading out to encompass every Dalek in the room.

The Daleks stirred, their voices rising in a cacophony of panic. "NO! WHAT IS... HAPPENING?!" they shrieked. "WE MUST... SURVIVE! WE ARE... THE DALEKS!"

The Doctor's eyes blazed as he held the shard steady. "You've had your chance," he said, his voice echoing with finality. "You've been given more lives than you deserve. But now, it's over. You are being erased from the cycle of time."

The light from the shard intensified, flooding the chamber with a blinding brilliance. The Daleks screamed, their voices twisting into distorted wails as their forms began to dissolve, breaking apart into particles of light and shadow. The chamber shook violently, and the Doctor braced himself, feeling the pull of the temporal energy as it severed the Daleks from the fabric of reality.

One by one, the Daleks disintegrated, their essence absorbed into the light that filled the room. The air grew warmer, the metallic scent dissipating as the last echoes of the Dalek Empire faded into silence.

The Doctor lowered the shard, breathing heavily as he surveyed the empty chamber. It was done. The Daleks had been erased, removed not just from the physical plane but from the cycle of existence. They would not return.

Kelnar approached cautiously, his eyes wide with disbelief. "You... you did it," he whispered. "They're gone."

The Doctor turned to him, exhaustion etched into his features. "Yes," he replied softly. "The Daleks are finally gone. I used the moth's energy to sever them from the time stream, ensuring they can never rise again."

Kelnar swallowed, a mixture of relief and sadness in his eyes. "But... was it worth it?"

The Doctor sighed, slipping the shard back into his pocket. "It's never easy," he admitted. "Erasing an entire species, even one as destructive as the Daleks, is a burden. But they posed a threat to the balance of the universe that couldn't be ignored. They would have continued to bring death and chaos if left unchecked. So yes, it was worth it, but it will weigh on me for the rest of my days."

He turned to leave the chamber, pausing at the threshold. "Come on, Kelnar," he said wearily. "There's still a universe out there that needs guidance. And it's up to us to ensure that what fills the void left by the Daleks is something better, something that values life over destruction."

As they made their way back through the caverns, the Doctor felt a sense of somber resolve. The Daleks were gone, their darkness erased from the universe's story. Now, the challenge lay in nurturing the light that would take their place, ensuring that balance could finally, truly, endure.

Chapter 23: The Cybermen's Defeat

The newly reborn world had a strange calmness to it, like the silence that follows a storm. The Death Moth had returned to the shadow world, the Daleks had been eradicated from the timeline, and the valley was flourishing with new life. However, the Doctor knew there was still one final threat to address—the last remnants of the Cybermen.

Standing on a hillside overlooking the sprawling landscape, the Doctor felt the weight of his task pressing down on him. The Cybermen, like the Daleks, were parasites on the universe, seeking to strip away life's diversity and turn everything into a reflection of their own cold, metallic existence. Their threat loomed over every timeline, always adapting, always seeking to convert and conquer.

Kelnar approached, his face drawn with concern. "Doctor," he began hesitantly, "You've already done so much. We've stopped the Master, eradicated the Daleks... Can't we rest now? The world is healing."

The Doctor shook his head, his eyes hardening as he scanned the horizon. "Not yet, Kelnar," he replied gravely. "The universe can't truly heal while the Cybermen remain. They're a contagion, a force that will continue to seek out new worlds to assimilate. I've fought them countless times, stopped them in numerous timelines, but they always find a way back. This time, we need to end it—permanently."

Kelnar nodded, though his expression remained worried. "How do we do that?" he asked. "They're even more adaptable than the Daleks."

The Doctor slipped his hands into his coat pockets, his gaze turning inward as he considered the problem. "The Cybermen are nothing if not persistent," he acknowledged. "But they're also predictable. They thrive on converting others, spreading their influence like a virus. However, that obsession is also their weakness. They're drawn to technological sources of power, especially ones that hold the promise of a new edge in their endless war."

A faint smile touched the Doctor's lips as an idea began to take shape in his mind. "We're going to set a trap, Kelnar," he said, his voice growing more confident. "One that will lure out the Cybermen's remaining forces and neutralize them once and for all."

Kelnar frowned, his curiosity piqued. "How do you plan to do that?"

The Doctor pulled out his sonic screwdriver and held it up, its tip glowing softly. "The Death Moth's energy left traces in the shadow world when it returned to its realm. I can use the residual energy here to create a signal that will mimic the presence of an advanced, unassimilated technology—a bait the Cybermen won't be able to resist."

"And when they come for it?" Kelnar asked, his voice wavering slightly.

The Doctor's eyes glinted with a mix of determination and sorrow. "When they come, I'll trigger a feedback loop using the moth's energy. It will create an electromagnetic pulse, combined with a temporal disruption, that will fry their systems and sever their connections to their network across time and space. No more resurrection, no more rebuilding."

Kelnar took a step back, understanding the gravity of what the Doctor was proposing. "You're going to destroy them completely?"

The Doctor nodded slowly. "Yes," he said, his voice heavy. "If we don't, they'll keep coming back, always adapting, always seeking to erase what makes life unique. This is the only way to stop them for good."

Kelnar hesitated, then nodded in agreement. "Alright, Doctor. I trust you. What do you need me to do?"

The Doctor smiled, a glimmer of gratitude in his eyes. "Just stay close and be ready to take cover. When the Cybermen arrive, things are going to get... hectic."

With Kelnar standing by, the Doctor worked quickly, using the sonic screwdriver to create a resonance field in the heart of the valley. The air began to shimmer faintly as the residual energy of the Death Moth coalesced, forming a beacon that pulsed with an enticing frequency—one that would call out to the Cybermen like a siren song.

"Now, we wait," the Doctor said, stepping back to observe his handiwork. "It won't take long for them to sense the signal."

As if on cue, a low, mechanical hum filled the air, growing louder with each passing moment. The Doctor's eyes narrowed as he scanned the horizon. From the shadows of the forest, a series of metallic figures emerged, marching in perfect unison. Their armor gleamed in the sunlight, reflecting the lifeless silver of their bodies. The Cybermen had arrived.

"Doctor, they're here," Kelnar whispered, his voice tight with fear.

"I see them," the Doctor replied, his expression unreadable. "Stay calm. This is the moment of truth."

The Cybermen continued their advance, their movements synchronized with an eerie precision. The lead Cyberman raised its arm, scanning the energy field the Doctor had created. "UNIDENTIFIED ENERGY SOURCE DETECTED," it droned in its hollow, mechanical voice. "POTENTIAL TECHNOLOGICAL ADVANTAGE. INITIATE ASSIMILATION PROTOCOL."

The Doctor stepped forward, his stance defiant. "You won't assimilate anything today," he called out. "This ends here, Cybermen. You've spent eons turning life into cold machinery, erasing everything that makes existence vibrant. No more."

The lead Cyberman turned its head, its eyepiece glowing a cold blue. "YOU ARE THE DOCTOR," it stated flatly. "YOU CANNOT STOP OUR ASCENSION. WE WILL ERASE ALL IMPERFEC-TION."

The Doctor's jaw tightened, and he raised his sonic screwdriver. "You talk about ascension, but all you bring is death," he retorted. "You've forgotten what it means to be alive, to change and grow. Well, today, I'm going to remind you that life isn't something you can simply convert into machinery."

He activated the sonic screwdriver, sending a pulse of energy into the resonance field. The air around them vibrated, a deep hum rising as the field began to react with the moth's residual energy. Light burst forth from the center of the field, a dazzling display of swirling colors and crackling electricity that spread out in a wave toward the Cybermen.

"WHAT IS HAPPENING?" the lead Cyberman demanded, its voice rising in alarm. "SYSTEMS... UNSTABLE. INITIATE... RE-BOOT."

The Doctor watched, his expression stern, as the wave of energy enveloped the Cybermen. Sparks flew from their armor, and the air filled with the sound of grinding metal and distorted electronic screams. The Cybermen convulsed, their movements becoming erratic as the feed-back loop disrupted their circuits and severed their connections to the hive mind.

"Doctor, it's working!" Kelnar shouted, his eyes wide with a mixture of horror and awe.

"Hold steady!" the Doctor called back, focusing intently on main-taining the field. "We need to ensure the temporal disruption severs their connection across all timelines!"

The Cybermen staggered, their once-impenetrable ranks now falling into disarray. The lead Cyberman lurched forward, its voice breaking into static. "YOU... CANNOT... STOP US... WE WILL... ADAPT..."

"Not this time," the Doctor replied coldly. "You've adapted to everything—except for this. The energy of the Death Moth isn't something you can assimilate. It's a force of balance, of life and death, and it will not be bent to your will."

The resonance field flared, sending out one final, massive pulse. The Cybermen let out a collective scream, their bodies convulsing as they were hit by the wave of energy. In an instant, their armor began to crack and crumble, disintegrating into fine particles of dust that scattered into the wind.

The Doctor lowered his sonic screwdriver, breathing heavily as he surveyed the scene. The field had dissipated, leaving behind only silence and the faint, echoing hum of residual energy. The Cybermen were gone.

Kelnar approached cautiously, his face pale. "Are... are they really gone?" he asked, his voice shaky.

The Doctor nodded, though his expression was somber. "Yes," he replied quietly. "The feedback loop severed their network and erased their essence from the timeline. They won't be coming back."

Kelnar exhaled, relief and sadness mingling in his eyes. "It's over then. The Cybermen, the Daleks... all of them."

The Doctor turned to face the horizon, his gaze distant. "For now, yes," he said. "The shadow world is restored, and the balance has been achieved. But the fight for balance is ongoing. There will always be forces seeking to disrupt it, to impose their will upon the universe."

He slipped the sonic screwdriver into his pocket and glanced at Kelnar. "But that's why we're here," he added, a faint smile tugging at the corners of his mouth. "To guide, to protect, to ensure that life continues to grow in all its beautiful, chaotic forms."

Kelnar nodded, a glimmer of hope returning to his eyes. "So, what now?"

The Doctor turned and began walking toward the edge of the valley, the sun casting a warm glow over the landscape. "Now, we move forward," he said. "There's a universe out there that needs shepherding, worlds that need healing. We carry the memory of what's been lost and use it to build something better."

As they walked away from the valley, leaving behind the remnants of the Cybermen's last stand, the Doctor felt a weight lift from his shoulders. The shadow world was restored, and the cosmic balance had been reclaimed. There would always be challenges ahead, new threats and old ones returning in different forms. But for now, they had achieved a victory that resonated through the fabric of the universe.

And as long as he drew breath, the Doctor would continue to fight for that balance, to protect the fragile beauty of life against the darkness that sought to consume it.

Chapter 24: The Doctor's Farewell

The sky above the shadow world had transformed from its once foreboding darkness into a vibrant expanse of swirling blues, pinks, and golds. Life flourished where the land had been barren, and the air hummed with the energy of renewal. The valley, which had once been a battlefield for the Death Moth, the Daleks, and the Cybermen, now teemed with signs of rebirth. Yet, despite the beauty around him, the Doctor felt the weight of recent events pressing heavily on his hearts.

He stood on a hilltop overlooking the valley, hands in his pockets, the tails of his coat fluttering gently in the breeze. Below, the people of the shadow world had gathered, their faces a mixture of awe, relief, and apprehension. They had witnessed both the devastation and the restoration of their world, guided through it all by the Doctor's steady hand.

Kelnar approached from behind, his footsteps soft on the grassy ground. "Doctor," he called, his voice breaking the silence. "It's almost time, isn't it?"

The Doctor nodded, though his gaze remained fixed on the horizon. "Yes," he replied quietly. "This world is healing, and my work here is done—for now. There are other places in the universe that need my help, other battles to fight."

Kelnar stopped beside him, looking out over the valley. "I can't believe it's finally over," he said, his voice tinged with disbelief. "The Death Moth, the Daleks, the Cybermen... it all seemed impossible to overcome. And yet, here we are."

The Doctor turned to face him, a sad smile crossing his face. "Balance is never easy, Kelnar," he said softly. "It demands sacrifices, hard choices, and the willingness to embrace both destruction and renewal. The Death Moth showed us that in the most profound way possible. Sometimes, to preserve life, something must fall to give room for new growth."

Kelnar lowered his gaze, his expression conflicted. "But at what cost? You gave up so much—your connection with the Death Moth, the promise of guiding it toward a future of renewal rather than destruction."

The Doctor sighed, running a hand through his hair. "Yes, I did," he admitted. "But it was necessary. The moth had to fulfill its role to restore the balance that the Daleks and Cybermen had disrupted. I couldn't be the one to dictate its path forever. It had to return to its nature, to ensure the universe continues on its cycle of growth and rebirth."

He paused, glancing up at the sky, where faint traces of the shadow world's past turmoil still lingered. "The cost is high," he continued, his voice growing distant. "But the universe is a vast, complex web of interconnected lives and forces. To maintain its balance, sometimes we must accept that not all endings are happy, not all sacrifices are fair. It's the burden of those who fight to protect it."

Kelnar looked at him, his eyes filled with gratitude and sadness. "And what about you, Doctor? What do you do now?"

The Doctor's smile returned, tinged with a mixture of melancholy and resolve. "Oh, you know me," he said, a hint of humor creeping into his voice. "I never stay in one place for long. There's always another crisis, another world in need of help. It's what I do."

He turned toward the gathering below, the people who had survived the upheavals of the shadow world. They watched him with a mix of admiration and anxiety, unsure of what his departure would mean for their future.

"It's time," the Doctor muttered, taking a deep breath. He began to walk down the hill, Kelnar following at his side. As they approached, the crowd parted, giving the Doctor space to address them.

"People of the shadow world," the Doctor called out, his voice carrying across the valley. "You've faced darkness and death, witnessed the brink of destruction, and now stand at the dawn of a new era. You've shown strength, resilience, and the capacity to grow beyond what you once were."

A murmur of agreement rippled through the crowd. Faces that had once been etched with fear now showed hope, though tinged with uncertainty. The Doctor looked at each of them, taking in the emotions swirling in their eyes.

"But this is not the end," he continued. "The shadow world is healing, yes, but maintaining that balance will be your task. I cannot stay to guide you, for there are others out there who need my help, just as you did. You must take what you've learned, the memories of what has passed, and use them to build a future that embraces life in all its forms."

An elderly woman stepped forward, her eyes moist with tears. "Will you come back if we need you, Doctor?" she asked, her voice quavering.

The Doctor approached her, placing a gentle hand on her shoulder. "If the universe permits it," he said kindly. "I will always come if you truly need me. But my hope is that you won't need me again—not because I don't want to return, but because you'll have grown strong enough to face whatever comes on your own."

He turned back to address the rest of the crowd. "The Death Moth has returned to its role in the cosmos, watching over the balance. Its memory, its influence, remains here in this world, reminding you of the lessons it imparted. Remember that life is not just about avoiding destruction, but about learning from it, about finding new ways to grow and thrive."

The people nodded, some wiping away tears, others standing with renewed determination. Kelnar stepped forward, his expression a mixture of sadness and admiration. "We will remember, Doctor," he vowed. "We'll carry the memory of the Death Moth and your guidance with us, and we'll strive to protect the balance you helped restore."

The Doctor gave a solemn nod. "Good," he said simply. "That's all I could ask for."

He reached into his pocket and pulled out his sonic screwdriver, turning it over in his hand thoughtfully. "Now, before I go," he added, his eyes sparkling with that familiar hint of mischief, "I think I should leave you with something useful."

He pointed the screwdriver at the ground, sending a beam of light that traced a circle in the earth. Within the circle, a faint glow began to emanate, pulsating softly like a heartbeat. "This is a beacon," the Doctor explained. "It's tuned to the shadow world's energy. Should you ever face a crisis that you can't handle alone, activate it, and it will send a signal. I'll come as fast as I can."

The crowd gasped, a murmur of gratitude sweeping through them. The elderly woman, her eyes now shining with hope, bowed her head. "Thank you, Doctor," she whispered. "For everything."

The Doctor smiled warmly. "No need for thanks," he replied. "Just promise me you'll look after each other. That's the true way to maintain balance—to care for the lives around you, to nurture them as you would a growing forest."

He stepped back, glancing at Kelnar, who had remained quiet, his eyes fixed on the Doctor. "Take care of them," the Doctor said to Kelnar. "You've seen the worst, and you've survived. Now, help them build the best."

Kelnar nodded, his voice choked with emotion. "I will, Doctor. I promise."

With a final look around, the Doctor turned and walked toward the TARDIS, which stood at the edge of the valley, its blue form gleaming in the sunlight. The crowd watched in silence as he approached, knowing that this moment marked the end of one chapter and the beginning of another.

He paused at the TARDIS door, turning back one last time. "Remember," he called out. "The universe is vast and filled with wonders. Don't let fear bind you. Seek out the light, the joy, and the possibility of what you can become."

With that, he stepped inside the TARDIS, the door closing behind him. A low hum filled the air, and the light atop the TARDIS began to pulse. The sound of the TARDIS's engines—the rhythmic wheezing and groaning—echoed through the valley as it slowly dematerialized, leaving behind only the rustling of leaves in the wind and the faint warmth of hope.

Kelnar stood among the crowd, his gaze fixed on the spot where the TARDIS had been. "He's gone," he said softly, almost to himself.

The elderly woman placed a hand on his arm, her eyes filled with quiet strength. "But his legacy remains," she replied. "We must honor that by nurturing this world and each other."

Kelnar nodded, feeling a surge of resolve. "Yes," he agreed. "We'll make this world flourish. For the Doctor, for the Death Moth, and for ourselves."

As the people of the shadow world dispersed, returning to their lives with renewed purpose, the valley itself seemed to breathe, alive with the promise of a future shaped by the lessons of the past. And though the Doctor had gone, his influence lingered, a guardian not of presence but of memory and guidance.

High above, the sky shimmered, a reminder that somewhere in the vast cosmos, the Doctor continued his journey. And as long as he roamed the stars, there would always be hope for balance, renewal, and the endless struggle to protect the light within the shadows.

Chapter 25: A New Beginning

The interior of the TARDIS hummed gently, the familiar rhythm soothing the Doctor as he stood at the console, his hands hovering over the controls. The recent events played over in his mind—defeating the Master, eradicating the Daleks, neutralizing the Cybermen, and guiding the shadow world through a period of profound transformation. It had been an arduous journey, one filled with tough choices and deep losses, but also moments of hope and triumph.

He took a deep breath, his gaze fixed on the monitor displaying the view of the valley outside. The people of the shadow world had already begun to scatter, returning to their lives, carrying with them the lessons of balance and renewal he had strived to impart. He felt a mixture of relief and sadness, knowing that his role here was at an end, at least for now.

"Well, old girl," the Doctor said, patting the TARDIS console fondly. "It's time for a new adventure. We've done our part here, and the universe is calling."

The TARDIS responded with a soft whirring sound, lights on the console flickering as if acknowledging his words. The Doctor smiled, taking comfort in the companionship of his ancient ship. Together, they had roamed the stars, danced through time, and faced down horrors. And now, they would once again embark on the unknown.

He began to flip a series of switches, inputting coordinates for their next destination. Somewhere, out there in the vastness of space and time, there was a new crisis to avert, a new world to explore, and new lives to touch. As the TARDIS engines groaned into life, the Doctor paused, glancing back at the screen that displayed the shadow world one last time.

The valley was bathed in the golden light of dawn, the shadows long and stretching across the newly grown fields and forests. Life had returned to the world, reborn from the ashes of chaos and destruction. It was a sight that filled the Doctor's hearts with both pride and a touch of sadness.

"Keep growing," he whispered to the world outside. "Remember the lessons, the sacrifices, and the hope. You've got a chance now. Make the most of it."

His fingers hovered over the final lever, ready to send the TARDIS back into the time vortex. But just as he was about to pull it, something outside caught his eye. He leaned closer to the monitor, squinting to make out a faint glimmer in the early morning light.

There, fluttering gently above the valley, was a single Death Moth.

The Doctor's breath hitched in his throat, his hearts skipping a beat. The moth hovered for a moment, its wings casting a soft glow in the dawn light. It was smaller than when he had last seen it, less an embodiment of cosmic force and more a quiet reminder—a symbol of balance that had been restored, for now.

He couldn't help but smile, a warm, bittersweet smile that held a world of emotions. "You're still here," he murmured. "Watching, guiding... keeping the balance."

The Death Moth seemed to pulse with light as if acknowledging his words. Then, with a graceful sweep of its wings, it drifted upward, higher into the sky, before vanishing into the early morning haze. Its presence left behind a lingering sense of peace and a subtle reminder that balance, while fragile, was something worth striving for.

The Doctor leaned back from the monitor, his eyes bright with renewed resolve. "Right, then!" he said, his voice echoing in the spacious control room. "No time to rest. There's a whole universe out there, and it's not going to look after itself."

He pulled the final lever, and the TARDIS engines roared to life, shaking the room as the ship prepared to dematerialize. Lights flickered, and the familiar grinding wheeze filled the air, signaling the TARDIS's departure from the shadow world. Outside, the blue box began to shimmer, fading in and out of existence, until with a final groan, it vanished completely, leaving behind only an empty space where it had stood.

The TARDIS hurtled through the time vortex, its form twisting and turning amidst the swirling colors and lights of the infinite. The Doctor moved around the console, adjusting dials and flipping switches, guiding the ship through the maelstrom of space and time. As he worked, his thoughts wandered to the journey that lay ahead.

"So, where to next?" he mused aloud, glancing up at the time rotor as it moved rhythmically. "A planet in peril? A civilization on the brink? A bit of sightseeing, perhaps?" He chuckled to himself, enjoying the limitless possibilities that lay before him.

He moved to the monitor, bringing up a star chart filled with the countless worlds and timelines they could visit. But as he scanned the chart, his mind kept drifting back to the shadow world and the single Death Moth he had seen before leaving. It was a symbol, a reminder that balance in the universe was a constant struggle, requiring vigilance and intervention. And sometimes, it demanded more than he was willing to give.

He paused, resting his hands on the edge of the console. "Balance," he muttered. "It's never easy, is it? It requires sacrifices, choices that leave marks on the heart. But it's also... beautiful in its way."

The TARDIS hummed softly, and the lights on the console dimmed slightly as if responding to his contemplations. He straightened up, his eyes brightening with determination. "Well, whatever comes next," he said, his voice firm, "we'll face it head-on, won't we, old girl? Because that's what we do. We wander the stars, we fight the darkness, and we protect the balance."

He reached out and spun the coordinate dial, letting it come to rest on a set of random, unexplored coordinates. With a flourish, he grabbed the lever and grinned. "Let's see where this takes us, then."

The TARDIS engines roared, and the ship surged forward through the vortex, leaving behind a trail of shimmering light. The Doctor held onto the console as the room shook around him, laughing with exhilaration. He was ready—ready for whatever awaited them at the next stop on their endless journey.

As the TARDIS hurtled onward, the Doctor cast one last glance at the screen, where the image of the shadow world had faded. His smile softened, filled with both nostalgia and hope. "You're in good hands now," he whispered to the memory of that world. "And if you ever need me... I'll be there."

The ship shuddered, lights flickering wildly as it sped toward its unknown destination. The Doctor took a deep breath, feeling the thrill of adventure, the call of the stars pulling him forward. The universe was vast, unpredictable, filled with dangers and wonders alike. And it was his to explore, to protect, to love.

Outside, amidst the swirling chaos of the time vortex, a faint glimmer appeared—a brief flash of light, like the fluttering of a moth's wings. It was gone in an instant, but it left behind a sense of reassurance, a reminder that somewhere, in the vast expanse of reality, balance was being watched over.

The Doctor smiled, his eyes gleaming with determination. "Onward!" he declared, pulling a lever to set the TARDIS on its new course. "Let's see what the universe has in store for us."

And so, the TARDIS sailed through the stars, carrying the Doctor to his next adventure, leaving behind the shadow world in a state of renewed hope. The single Death Moth had been a sign—a promise that balance had been restored, for now. But the Doctor knew that the struggle was never truly over. It would continue, as long as life existed, as long as there were those willing to fight for the light in the darkness.

With a flash, the TARDIS vanished into the endless possibilities of space and time, the Doctor at the helm, ready for whatever awaited him next. The universe held its breath, its guardian moving forward, ever vigilant, ever hopeful, always striving to keep the balance alive.

And somewhere, in the depths of the cosmos, the flutter of wings echoed—a quiet testament that the light would endure.

<u>Message from the Author:</u>

I hope you enjoyed this book, I love astrology and knew there was not a book such as this out on the shelf. I love metaphysical items as well. Please check out my other books:

-Life of Government Benefits

-My life of Hell

-My life with Hydrocephalus

-Red Sky

-World Domination:Woman's rule

-World Domination:Woman's Rule 2: The War

-Life and Banishment of Apophis: book 1

-The Kidney Friendly Diet

-The Ultimate Hemp Cookbook

-Creating a Dispensary(legally)

-Cleanliness throughout life: the importance of showering from childhood to adulthood.

-Strong Roots: The Risks of Overcoddling children

-Hemp Horoscopes: Cosmic Insights and Earthly Healing

- Celestial Hemp Navigating the Zodiac: Through the Green Cosmos

-Astrological Hemp: Aligning The Stars with Earth's Ancient Herb

-The Astrological Guide to Hemp: Stars, Signs, and Sacred Leaves

-Green Growth: Innovative Marketing Strategies for your Hemp Products and Dispensary

-Cosmic Cannabis

-Astrological Munchies

-Henry The Hemp

-Zodiacal Roots: The Astrological Soul Of Hemp

- **Green Constellations: Intersection of Hemp and Zodiac**

-Hemp in The Houses: An astrological Adventure Through The Cannabis Galaxy

-Galactic Ganja Guide

Heavenly Hemp

Zodiac Leaves

Doctor Who Astrology

Cannastrology

Stellar Satvias and Cosmic Indicas

Celestial Cannabis: A Zodiac Journey

AstroHerbology: The Sky and The Soil: Volume 1

AstroHerbology:Celestial Cannabis:Volume 2

Cosmic Cannabis Cultivation

The Starry Guide to Herbal Harmony: Volume 1

The Starry Guide to Herbal Harmony: Cannabis Universe: Volume 2

Yugioh Astrology: Astrological Guide to Deck, Duels and more

Nightmare Mansion: Echoes of The Abyss

Nightmare Mansion 2: Legacy of Shadows

Nightmare Mansion 3: Shadows of the Forgotten

Nightmare Mansion 4: Echoes of the Damned

The Life and Banishment of Apophis: Book 2

Nightmare Mansion: Halls of Despair

Healing with Herb: Cannabis and Hydrocephalus
Planetary Pot: Aligning with Astrological Herbs: Volume 1
Fast Track to Freedom: 30 Days to Financial Independence Using AI, Assets, and Agile Hustles
Cosmic Hemp Pathways
How to Become Financially Free in 30 Days: 10,000 Paths to Prosperity
Zodiacal Herbage: Astrological Insights: Volume 1
Nightmare Mansion: Whispers in the Walls
The Daleks Invade Atlantis
Henry the hemp and Hydrocephalus

10X The Kidney Friendly Diet
Cannabis Universe: Adult coloring book
Hemp Astrology: The Healing Power of the Stars
Zodiacal Herbage: Astrological Insights: Cannabis Universe: Volume 2
Planetary Pot: Aligning with Astrological Herbs: Cannabis Universes: Volume 2
Doctor Who Meets the Replicators and SG-1: The Ultimate Battle for Survival
Nightmare Mansion: Curse of the Blood Moon
The Celestial Stoner: A Guide to the Zodiac
Cosmic Pleasures: Sex Toy Astrology for Every Sign
Hydrocephalus Astrology: Navigating the Stars and Healing Waters
Lapis and the Mischievous Chocolate Bar

Celestial Positions: Sexual Astrology for Every Sign
Apophis's Shadow Work Journal: : A Journey of Self-Discovery and Healing
Kinky Cosmos: Sexual Kink Astrology for Every Sign
Digital Cosmos: The Astrological Digimon Compendium
Stellar Seeds: The Cosmic Guide to Growing with Astrology

Apophis's Daily Gratitude Journal

Cat Astrology: Feline Mysteries of the Cosmos
The Cosmic Kama Sutra: An Astrological Guide to Sexual Positions
Unleash Your Potential: A Guided Journal Powered by AI Insights
Whispers of the Enchanted Grove

Cosmic Pleasures: An Astrological Guide to Sexual Kinks
369, 12 Manifestation Journal
Whisper of the nocturne journal(blank journal for writing or drawing)
The Boogey Book
Locked In Reflection: A Chastity Journey Through Locktober
Generating Wealth Quickly:
How to Generate $100,000 in 24 Hours
Star Magic: Harness the Power of the Universe
The Flatulence Chronicles: A Fart Journal for Self-Discovery

If you want solar for your home go here: https://www.harborsolar.live/apophisenterprises/

Get Some Tarot cards: https://www.makeplayingcards.com/sell/apophis-occult-shop

<u>Get some shirts: https://www.bonfire.com/store/apophis-shirt-emporium/</u>

<u>Instagrams:</u>
@apophis_enterprises,

@apophisbookemporium,
@apophisscardshop
Twitter: @apophisenterpr1 Tiktok:@apophisenterprise
Youtube: @sg1fan23477, @FiresideRetreatKingdom Top of
Form

Podcast: Apophis Chat Zone: https://open.spotify.com/show/5zXbrCLEV2xzCp8ybrfHsk?si=fb4d4fdbdce44dec

Newsletter: https://apophiss-newsletter-27c897.beehiiv.com/